6/16

END GAME

END GAME

ALAN GIBBONS

Indigo

Orion Children's Books

First published in Great Britain in 2015 by Hodder and Stoughton
This edition first published in Great Britain in 2016 by Hodder and
Stoughton

10 9 8 7 6 5 4 3 2 1

Text copyright © Alan Gibbons 2015

The moral rights of the author and illustrator have been asserted.

A CIP catalogue record for this book
is available from the British Library.

ISBN: 978 1 78062 181 4

Typeset by Input Data Services Ltd, Bridgwater, Somerset

Printed and bound by Clays Ltd, St Ives plc

The paper and board used in this book are
made from wood from responsible sources.

MIX
Paper from
responsible sources
FSC
www.fsc.org
FSC® C104740

For Malala Yousafzai
and all who work
for girls'
education

DEAD EYES

He was here again last night, the man with the dead eyes.

He was in my room.

He was in my head.

I don't have a name for him yet. I don't have names for many things since it happened. What I have is a jumble. Cluttered images steal into my thoughts. I don't know which are real and which are dreams and nightmares, which ones might explain what I'm doing here and which are figments of my imagination. I don't know how to put them into any kind of order. It's as if time has ruptured, spilling its entrails on the floor where they steam and slide. Events from the past slither this way and that, tangled, oily, chaotic.

Nothing makes sense.

I know this man is important, the one with the dead eyes. I'd like to believe he's a monster, the creation of some dark corner of my mind. But he comes to stand at the bottom of my bed. Sometimes he just waits and watches. Then there are the times when he screams. Strangely, there's no sound when he does, just the sight of his mouth. It gapes so wide I can imagine the flesh tearing in the corners to leave a bloody maw.

There's a famous painting of a scream, but that's a kind of twisted pain, a moan of desperation. This is hatred. It's savage and it's directed at me. It's as if my mind is a jigsaw, hundreds, thousands of pieces of memory that somebody has tossed into the air. They fall to the floor, scattering this way and that. I hope it is a fantasy. What if I'm right and he's real? What if the man who comes to stand at the foot of my bed isn't just some macabre ghost? What if he's flesh and blood like me?

Since this happened, I have been immune to any kind of sensation. I'm an automaton, impervious to the physical world. There's no heat or cold, no draught blowing from the door or window, no throb of pain, no dull ache, not even the slightest tickle or itch. I feel neither softness nor moisture.

Memories stutter: a car driven too fast, hands, *my*

hands on the steering wheel. My knuckles are white from gripping too tightly. I don't remember many things, but my name is there among the debris. It's Mallory, Nick Mallory. I know how old I am. I've just turned seventeen. Other than that, there isn't much to tell. I came out of the car broken. I'm pretty much a blank page. What's going on here? How can I have clear memories of some things and total confusion about others? Life is meant to have a pattern, isn't it?

The storm of questions turns into a blizzard. I find myself grasping at them like a child trying to catch snowflakes. One last, fragile crystal trembles as it starts to melt. It's this. What would Nick Mallory, a seventeen-year-old sixth former, be doing in a car on an unlit lane, going at sixty miles an hour? Yes, that's another of the pieces. I can hear the rush of acceleration. I can see the speedo. I'm driving the Beemer at sixty miles an hour on a road that's little more than a potholed track. The headlights probe the darkness, but make little impression.

The Beemer.

There, that's another detail slotting into place. This isn't just any car. It's a BMW 7 Series. We're talking about a vehicle with a fifty-thousand-pound price tag. That's something else I know about Nick Mallory. His daddy's rich and his momma's good-looking. Oh great, now I'm thinking in song lyrics. That's one my grandparents are always playing. I'm losing it, falling back into confusion. Some things don't even amount to memories, just fragments. There are snatches of music. Songs, scraps of experience haunt the deadening nightmare.

Back to the car. It's a three-litre, straight six turbo-diesel. It can go from standstill to sixty miles per hour in less than seven seconds and that's what I did the night of the accident, accelerated to shattering, destructive impact. Well, way to go, Nicky boy. That's vandalism of the highest order. I left a beautiful piece of German engineering trashed against a hundred-year-old oak tree on the last bend before the lane opens on to a winding country road just outside . . .

. . . outside . . .

. . . crap . . .

I've forgotten. How does that happen? I don't even know where I live any more! It's nestling in one of those confused piles of jigsaw pieces. That's all I have right now: my name, my age and the car I wrote off. I relive those crazy, careering moments, trying to make sense of what happened. It feels more like a computer game than a genuine memory. The road is blurry. Shadows dance and race and flash as the beams of the headlights slash the darkness.

There's a killer on the road . . .

Whoa, where did that come from?

You know what? I don't even want to know. I'm tired. I rest, though I'm unable to close my eyes. That's been worrying me. My gaze is fixed. I examine my surroundings: the wall-mounted television, the olive-coloured blinds to my left, the white walls, the sink and soap dispenser, the peeling poster reminding staff to wash their hands thoroughly. I've memorised every detail. It doesn't take long when it's all you've got to look at.

To my right there's a door. It hasn't opened. The ceiling has a crack. It's been filled clumsily and meanders across the plaster like a varicose vein. The strip light buzzes slightly and the light is yellowish. It flickers intermittently as if it's got a nervous tic. The plastic cover is dirty and there's a dead bluebottle at one end.

There are one or two other things: the IV drip snaking from its T-shaped metal stand, the fluid bag and pump, the turquoise curtains dangling from a plastic track. These are the mundane details of my hospital room. It's been this way since I recovered consciousness. To my surprise, I feel no sense of panic. You'd think I'd be experiencing all kinds of terror, that I'd be tumbling down a dark well of despair, but I'm content somehow, even comfortable with my lot. It suits me to be here, in this bed, attached to this line, this machine. Right now, there's nowhere I'd feel safer.

I've become increasingly convinced that this condition, this state of non-being, is preferable to what I was going through before the crash. I don't feel the slightest bit curious about the person I was before I drove that car into a tree. I only know that at this moment I would rather be anybody else in the whole wide world than Nick Mallory.

■

Something's changed since I drifted off. I rummage through the jumble that's been littering my mind, then I have it. The window to my left is a little hazy, part of that strange shadow world just outside my core vision, but I can tell that it's dark outside.

I must have been asleep for some time, a couple of hours at least. Fancy that, it seems I can sleep with my eyes open. That's a neat trick, a bit like the way cows and horses sleep standing up. The level in the fluid bag has changed too. Somebody's replaced it while I was dozing. So the nurse has been in. I'm not sure what to think about that. There's something creepy about lying here while people slip in and out of my room, shove needles in my veins, feed tubes into my nostrils, hook me up to monitors. They see you while you're sleeping. They see you when you wake. The thought creeps me out. Does Dead Eyes watch me while I doze? Is he there at the end of my bed?

I wonder what the nurse is like. When's she going to appear? I say she, but it could be a man, of course. The door opens. Maybe this is the nurse now. The draught excluder purrs on the tiled floor. At first,

I don't see anyone, just the hint of a shadow. Then there he is, a tall, broad-shouldered man in his forties. He's instantly familiar. He's lean, muscular, square-chinned. It isn't the nurse. It's my father. Somebody rises to greet him. I hear the scrape of the chair legs.

The second person in the room is my mum. She must have been out of sight somewhere, behind my right shoulder. I realise that she's been there all the time. She's been holding an anguished vigil over her broken son. That's what mums do. She's spent hours by my side.

I remember now. She was holding my hand earlier, willing me to show some sign that I recognised her. Not that I could feel her touch. Like I said, I don't feel anything.

Now my father's talking. His words are directed over my head, to her.

'Is there any change?'

'No,' Mum says. 'None.'

Odd, that. I call her Mum as you'd expect, but I just called him *my father*. What *would* make me draw a distinction like that? It should be Mum and Dad surely. It's such a neat little phrase. It trips off the tongue, a kind of reflex. So why does the thought of calling this man Dad stick in my throat? If I could speak I know I'd choke on the word. It's palpable, this distance between us.

There's a word for the divide. It's . . . darkness.

A picture forms in my head. In the eerie half-light, we're both weighted down at the bottom of a pool. The sides are filthy. The surface is milky with scum. There are rust stains, chipped tiles, floating debris. It's hard to describe the full horror of this underwater world. We're struggling and kicking for our lives and there's all this black ink, billowing from an old rusting pipe. It stains the pool, enveloping us. Is it real? Or is it some kind of crazy, bad dream? My father interrupts my search for an answer.

'What did the doctor say?'

'Only that he would have to monitor Nick's progress and that he's stable. I don't know what more we can expect.'

'That's it? That's all he told you? Christ, Olivia, why do these people have to talk in platitudes? Of course they're monitoring Nick's progress. That's what they're bloody well paid for. And stable, what does that even mean?'

He stands there, shaking his head at nobody in particular. This is a man who is used to commanding attention. Everything about him oozes confidence and authority, but he is diminished.

'My son is lying there,' he murmurs, 'and I can't get any answers.'

His grief is unmistakable, but is there something else? A streak of brittleness, a sense of being on the edge that doesn't just seem to be about me alone. He is shifting responsibility.

'Please, Tim,' Mum says. 'You have to calm down. I know you're worried, but it won't do any good blaming the medical staff. They're doing what they can.'

She says lots of other things, stuff about my medication, the songs she's been singing to me, the things she's brought to stimulate my memory. She brandishes a photo album. It's maroon and laminated. One by one, she introduces me to the back pages of my life. She must have been hoping I would recall some key moment of my childhood.

Well, I do. I remember Mum. I remember my father. I remember my sister, Saffi. That's short for Saffron. She's thirteen, four years younger than me. Maybe that's why she isn't with them. There are long shadows on the wall facing me. They don't want her staying up late. Listen to Mr Responsible, he's lying on a hospital bed, all mushed up, and he's wondering about his little sister. Next thing you know, I'll be doing charity walks and wearing a coloured ribbon on my lapel.

I'm forming an impression of loving, indulgent, protective parents and a son who maybe doesn't deserve them. Or maybe he deserves one of them . . .

Or maybe . . .

Or maybe I don't know what the hell I'm talking about. It could be that they don't want Saffi seeing me like this. I wonder what *this* is. It didn't occur to me until now, but I have no idea what I look like. Nobody's thought to provide me with a mirror. Maybe it's for the best. I would have to be a masochist to want to see myself in this state.

Stop feeling sorry for yourself, Nick Mallory. It could be worse.

No, wait, it couldn't.

Because there's a killer on the road.

I'm still in this weird state of suspension. Does it mean I'm badly injured? Will I be able to walk again, play sport? Am I disfigured? It should worry me, the absence of pain, the possibility of long-term damage. If you're broken, shouldn't you feel something? Could it be the drugs? That might explain the numbness, the sense of floating inside myself, being detached. It could even explain the way I don't seem to care. Maybe they've pumped me so full of painkillers I'm in a world of my own.

That gets me thinking. If that's the reason I don't care, it's a bit scary. There will come a moment when they reduce the dose and I will start to feel again. There's a screamer on the bed. Suddenly, I'm anxious. How will I cope? I'm not brave. I'm terrified of pain. It isn't just a matter of one bone or even a few bones.

Every bit of me is broken.

It's hard to imagine how I would endure pain that bad, pain that was unbearable, pain that made me twist and turn, moan and scream and wish I was dead, pain that was a permanent feature of my life, an ever-present curse. But that time is far off. Right now, I can't blink, never mind twist and turn. There's safety in not feeling.

Mum's speaking.

'There's something I don't understand.'

My father turns his head, but doesn't say a word. He leaves the talking to Mum.

'What was he doing in the car?'

I watch my father. He doesn't respond. He doesn't even make eye contact with her. Mum voices her frustration.

'Tim, you must have an idea.'

My father's explanation is less than comprehensive.

'The keys were on the hall table. He must have taken them.'

Must have?

'But why? Why would he do that? It doesn't make any sense. He's only just started taking lessons. He's still on a provisional licence, for Christ's sake!' She realises she's shouting and struggles to compose herself. 'Look, the two of you were alone in the house when it happened. You must know things?'

There's a slight delay then he answers in a flat, even tone, so matter-of-fact it could sound dismissive.

'There was nothing. I was in the study. I didn't even know Nick was back. I was at my desk, going through casework, then I heard the engine start.

For a second, I thought somebody must be stealing the car.'

He was at his desk . . . then the engine started. No, that's not right. That's not the way it was. But how was it? I'm sure he saw me take the keys. He shouted. Yes, he yelled for me to stop. I'm flailing through the swirling memories, snatching at the debris. All I know is, he's missing things out, a whole load of things, the most important things.

Mum pulls her chair closer to the bed and sits down.

'You should never have let him near that car.'

'Olivia, is this some kind of accusation?' When there's no answer, he continues. 'Are you saying I did something wrong encouraging him to drive? Nick's seventeen. All his friends are learning.'

He waits for Mum to say something. She doesn't. Again he continues.

'He's a bright lad. He was picking it up really quickly.'

Mum's looking at him.

'Well, he didn't pick it up quickly enough, did he? He's just smashed your precious car into that tree. Why the hell did you leave the keys hanging around where he could find them?'

'Why wouldn't I? I didn't expect this to happen.'

Mum isn't listening.

'Look at the state he's in. What I don't understand

is why he was going so fast. He wasn't even wearing a seatbelt.'

That's right, I wasn't. I remember the protesting yelp of the device reminding me to put it on. Next up, it's the self-destruction derby. Thrills. Spills. Broken bones. There's no lighting on that stretch. There never was. If that's not a death wish, I don't know what is. I watch my father's body language, the way he lets his arms flop by his sides. Mum's watching him too. There's something wrong with my father's reaction. She knows it. I know it.

'Isn't there anything you can tell me? A seventeen-year-old boy doesn't just take off without cause. He's a sensible, well-balanced kid.'

Is that right? Nick Sensible. Balance Boy. Go me!

'He's never done anything like this before.'

My father's answer is composed.

'If there was anything I could say to explain this, I would.'

Now Mum's the one who takes time forming her words.

'Would you, Tim? Would you really?'

He kneels beside her. I notice the way he tugs at the knees of his trousers, hitching them up a little. He slips his arm round her shoulder and rests his forehead against hers. Fine, my parents love each other.

'There are no more secrets, Olivia. I promise.' He takes her hand and holds it for a long time before he speaks again. 'All I want is for our son to get better.'

The recrimination is gone. Mum clings to him.

'Oh Tim, I'm so scared. What if . . . ?'

Great. Now we're into the What If game. What if I'm beyond repair? What if I spend the rest of my life in a chair, sucking on a straw?

'Don't think like that. Nick's strong. He's going to make a full recovery.'

Mum smiles weakly. 'How's Saffi doing?'

'She's worried about Nick,' he says, 'but she's a good kid.' Pride shines in his face. I remember that glow. I would do anything to hear my name and see that look on his face. 'She's tougher than we give her credit for.'

I'm strong. Saffi's tough. What kind of kids did this guy raise, the Indestructibles?

My father's still talking.

'I dropped her off at Mum and Dad's. They'll make sure she gets to school.'

That seems to placate Mum.

'Did she ask about seeing Nick?'

'Yes. I said we'd arrange something this week.'

I don't register the remainder of their conversation. It fades into the background and becomes part of the noise of the hospital, like the gurgle of water in the radiators, the staccato tap of shoes in the corridor outside, the occasional wail of sirens, the rumble of traffic on the main road beyond the hospital gates.

None of this matters, not my parents, not Saffi,

not their discussions with the medical staff about my health. There's only one thing I care about and that's why I don't trust my father.

I find myself turning it over and over in my mind, trying to make sense of it all, but there's something stopping me. Not something, *someone*.

The killer on the road.

He has crept back into the room while they were speaking. Now he's standing at the bottom of my bed, his mouth wide open.

It's the man with the dead eyes.

WHAT'S NORMAL?

This time I think I'm alone. I can't be one hundred per cent certain. It's hard to be sure of anything when I keep moving through layers of numbness. Time seems to ebb and flow, sometimes freezing, sometimes racing. The only thing that doesn't move, doesn't shift, is static, is me. I'm the dead centre of this crazy world. I lie here and things happen to me. I'm unable to turn my head, find any perspective other than a fixed image of the wall opposite. I've got no sense of the room apart from what's immediately in front of me. It bewilders me that human life can shrink to this, a few square metres of wall and a TV screen. Mum blind-sided me the last time she visited. When was that, minutes ago, hours? Is this even the same day? The last thing I remember is my father trying to persuade Mum to go home and get some sleep.

'You look exhausted,' he said. 'Listen, Olivia, I know you don't want to leave Nick's side, but it isn't going to help him if you make yourself ill.'

Mum tries to say something but he gently places his finger on her lips.

'He needs us to be strong. You need some rest. The hospital will call us if there's any change.'

The nurse was in the room during the conversation. She nodded in agreement, mumbled something about Mum having to be there for me. Mum finally agreed to leave, but not before she expressed her concern about my condition.

'I don't like the way he just stares like that. He doesn't even blink.'

She's right, I don't. I am a camera, a lens through which the world filters. The nurse says something about trauma, explains that they've been putting drops in my eyes so they don't dry out, but that isn't what Mum means. It's not my vision that worries her. It's my brain.

'What if he's damaged? What if . . . ?'

She starts to cry. Each sob tears through her, hacking at her chest.

'You hear of such awful things, people who linger for years, not really living, but unable to die.'

Way to go, Mum. You really know how to cheer somebody up. The nurse seeks to reassure her.

'Nothing untoward is showing up on the scans,' she says.

Untoward? Is that a word? Un-to-ward. It sounds like an owl speaking a foreign language.

'Would you like to discuss it with the doctor?'

Mum shakes her head. 'No, that's OK. I've had all the medical jargon I can handle for one day.'

You and me both, Mum. The nurse smiles understandingly. She's pretty, Asian I think, sleek, black hair framing delicate features. But back to what Mum said.

'I just want my Nick back. I want him to come out of this . . . normal.'

I know what she's trying to say. She wants me to walk again, be able to speak clearly and articulately, have no visible reminders of the accident. Let's hear it for Normal Nicky, the kid who declared war on a tree and came up smiling. I know where Mum's coming from, of course. What parent wouldn't want the same for their child? The problem is, shrieking out of the confusion like some banshee comes the suspicion that what I had before the crash was anything but normal.

Something broke and I broke with it.

I spend the next few moments trying to unravel my thought processes. What is it about the life of Nick Mallory I'm so keen to reject?

OK, I don't quite remember why I'm angry with my father, but I am, *bloody* angry.

You know that perfect life you want me to return to, Mum? I'm not even sure it ever existed. A promo video is running, a computerised slideshow of my life complete with sliding panels, dissolves and shatter frames. In one, I'm lounging on the school field with a couple of mates, a tall, geeky kid and a Chinese boy. In another, I'm ploughing through mud, powering towards the line as I search for the winning try. I'm swimming, gliding through the water with golden sunlight rippling around me.

Other times, I'm curled up in a black leather armchair with a Lee Child or Stephen King on my lap. That's two books you won't get on the A level syllabus any time soon. It doesn't feel like such a bad life, but somehow it's a lie. That was then and this is now. The upshot of that high-speed drive is I just might not have any future.

Mum isn't much different to my father when it comes to the dream of perfection. They need the family wonderful, Mum, Dad and two scrubbed, smiling, healthy kids, but life has a habit of interfering with your dreams. It can put a thumb mark on a freshly painted surface or stick a footprint in newly laid concrete.

I remember one time my father took me with him on a hospital visit. He had tried to talk me out of it, but I was determined to go. He was talking to a group of wounded soldiers, fresh back from Afghanistan. I'll never forget the torn bodies, the faces tense with pain, the stumps where limbs had been. One guy had suffered appalling injuries. He had lost an eye, a hand, a leg. Is that what the future has in store for me, Nick Mallory, imprisoned in a mangled torso, head tilted to one side, struggling to communicate with his loved ones?

I loved my father so much that day, as we drove back from the hospital. He had talked to every man, listened carefully to their stories, shared his own memories of being in uniform. He managed to stay in touch with every one of them, remembering the names of their wives and kids, occasionally attending some important family event. He got that poor, destroyed man laughing and understanding he still had a family who loved him. He embraced that guy and they cried together. He cared, you see.

New images join the gallery of jumbled pictures hanging on the walls of my mind. They're the ones Mum showed me earlier. Earlier? Does that mean earlier today or was it yesterday? It's hard to make sense of time. There are none of the mundane, daily rituals that hold most people's lives together. I'm fed by a drip so I can't even look forward to mealtimes to break up the monotony.

Breakfast is a drip.

Lunch is a drip.

My tea is another lousy drip.

As for supper?

A drip.

Now and then I'm aware of the light dimming outside, but that's about it. When did the accident happen? Monday, I think. Or was it Tuesday? That would make today . . . Oh, what's the point? If I can't even remember when I hit that tree, how can I count forward and work out what day it is now?

Instead of torturing myself with pointless anxieties about what day it is, I summon each of the photos Mum showed me, one by one. The first makes me laugh. At least it would if I was capable of laughter. What possessed her to bring it? I'm two or three years old in the picture, sitting on the beach with the tide coming in. The water is lapping around my toes and splashing over my chubby little legs. The sun is on my face and I am utterly carefree.

I was happy then, still an only child, doted on, adored, the centre of my parents' universe. Everything is so simple when you're little. Your mum and dad tower over you. They're perfect, like gods. But they're not perfect, are they, not perfect at all.

When I see that boy with his tousled hair, sitting in the sand, I'd never think he was somebody riding for a fall. He thinks he will always be as happy as he is at that moment. He thinks his parents will always be there to pick him up. They will always be at hand with a ready smile and a warm kiss. They will never let him down.

Except they do.

The door opens and the nurse appears. It's her again, the pretty Asian woman.

'How are you doing?' she asks.

I want to turn round and check whether she's talking to me. I want to be De Niro in *Taxi Driver*. Are you looking at me? Maybe there's somebody lurking behind me again, sitting silently out of sight the way Mum did.

'I know you can hear me, Nick.'

So she *is* talking to me. It comes as a shock to have her addressing me directly, like I'm a human being, not a piece of shredded meat on a slab. I hate having to lie here while people discuss me as if I don't exist.

'It's a fine evening outside, a bit chilly but at least it isn't raining again. Have you seen those terrible floods on the news, Nick?'

Oh, she's good. She's very good. She knows the TV is my only window to the world.

'I hate the rain. It stops you doing anything.' She checks the IV, still chatting away in that relaxed, informal way of hers as if she's a family friend, not the nurse. 'Your mum will be back in the morning. I recognised her immediately, of course. I've seen her in magazines. I'd love to be that tall. Those legs! All my friends call me Short and Mighty.'

My mum is in the magazines? OK, that's news.

'She used to glide down the catwalk.'

Got it. She's either a model . . . or a cat. The nurse finishes tinkering with the IV and looks me right in the eye.

'I know your dad too. I've seen him on *Question Time*. My mum thinks he's hot.'

She doesn't say what she thinks about him.

'You're lucky to have such famous, talented parents.'

Yes, lucky, that's me. The door goes again and somebody leans in. She's plump, and fiftyish. She says something incomprehensible to do with another patient and scurries off down the corridor.

'Looks like I have to go,' my nurse says.

I manage to get a look at her nametag. She's Nurse Choudhury. Goodnight, Nurse Choudhury. The nurses must be told to talk to the patients like that. It might be a way of stimulating the patient's mind. I don't care about the medical reasons behind it. I like her talking to me. I like the soft, natural way she slips from one subject to another. There's no hidden agenda. There are no secrets.

With my parents, nothing's ever simple. Every moment Mum is here, she's on the verge of tears. I want to reach out and tell her everything will be OK. Then there's the way I feel when my father's around and everything sours.

It's fairly new, this fierce sense of loathing. I didn't hate him when I was little. I would remember.

I would feel it. That little boy on the beach, he giggled with delight when his daddy scooped him up. Not all the photos Mum held up for me brought the memories back, but one did. It showed the three of us on an airfield somewhere. My father was dressed in his Army uniform and he had me hoisted on his shoulders. I must have been four, maybe five at a stretch. Mum had one arm round my father's waist and the other supporting me and we were all laughing.

There were other service families in the background, but we were oblivious to them. Not one of us was looking into the camera lens. The whole thing was so perfect. We were happy then. You can't fake a scene as natural as this. So what happened to change it? Where did it come from, this sense of disappointment, so all-consuming I feel as if I'm choking?

You don't start hating your parents for nothing. Maybe if I was to really push it, to dig deep down into this weird scrapyard of a mind, I would come up with something, but I don't want to. It feels as if I'm tiptoeing through the wreckage left behind after the crash. There are all these bits and pieces lying around on the ground and I'm sidestepping them, afraid to pick them up, terrified of what I might find underneath.

I'm curious and scared, compelled and apprehensive all at the same time. Right here, in this room, in this hospital, I'm safe. I'm cocooned in my own paralysis. So long as I lie here, nailed down in the coffin of this body, I don't have to come to terms with anything.

I can live in the past. I can pick and choose which photos to recall, which relics of my childhood I will dust off and display. So far I have two. If I go slowly, taking care not to choose any that will open doors in my mind, I can be at peace with myself. So I stick with these two. The little boy on the beach is loved. The kid on his dad's shoulders is safe and secure. His father is a hero.

This is normal.

Normal.

Perfect.

An illusion.

■

How long have I been asleep? It's dark outside, but it isn't quiet. A hospital is a place that never sleeps. Trolleys rattle, machines bleep, heating systems hum. Conversation rumbles away in corridors. Soft-soled shoes pad along tiled floors.

Sometimes shadows creep round the flicker of a street lamp. Later, silhouetted twigs wave at the edge of my vision like the fingers of a charred hand. Then the sun rises again. Birdsong swells. The world turns. The light changes. I remain the same.

I am free of the constraints of time. I float, ageless,

rootless. It's as if I have fallen through a crack in the universe. I can be anywhere and any moment I want. One minute I'm three years old sitting on a beach, the next I'm seventeen, running from a man with dead eyes. A chair scrapes. Mum's back. She seems to sense that I am too.

'Are you awake, Nicky? You've just missed your dad.'

She has hold of my hands. I can't feel her touch, of course. Nothing's changed there.

'Gran and Grandad are bringing Saffi tomorrow. You'll like that. I know how close the two of you are.'

She continues in this vein for ten, fifteen, twenty minutes. She's got some music on her phone and puts it close to my ear. I listen to her telling me this is one of my favourite tracks. I don't have any choice in the matter of course. She could insert the SIM in my brain and I wouldn't be able to stop her. The playlist buzzes away.

So why do I want her to hit the stop button? I don't want music. I don't want talk. I don't want *her*. I hate being reminded of my old life. I don't want her kind of normal. What I want is ... What do I want? Maybe I want all this broken-up stuff inside me to make sense, but there is no sense. Anything remotely coherent in my life shattered into bits against that oak tree.

Next time I come to, it's getting light. I recognise

the grey, muddy tones of a winter's morning. Mum turns to the window and listens to the dawn chorus.

'I'm going now, Nick.'

She leans forward and presses a kiss on my forehead.

'You will get better, my boy. I know you will fight. Come back to us, Nicky, soon. We love you so much.'

She slips on a leather jacket, buttons it and walks to the door. As she leaves, there's somebody there to take her place. The man with the dead eyes. He stands at the bottom of my bed and the screaming starts. I can hear Mum's stilettos clicking down the corridor.

That's not normal.

This is normal.

DON'T RUN!

It was the blood that made me run.

I couldn't go back inside. A man was kneeling, hands clasped to his face. The blood was spurting, pumping in scarlet streams through his fingers, running down his arms, hot and bright. I could hear him gasping, gagging on the salty liquid. He was crushing his hands against his face, trying to staunch the blood.

'You betrayed them! You sick, self-obsessed liar, you betrayed them.'

There. This time it's my voice, echoing through the house, shriller, higher than it usually is. Moments earlier, other voices had broken the silence. It was two men. These voices were raised. They had been fighting for attention, beating each other down. A dogfight, that's what it was. Now they were quieter. A man was groaning, struggling for breath.

'You've broken my nose. Is that what you do to somebody who tells the truth, you break his nose?'

Stop whining, you think you've got problems? My father broke your nose. Try to imagine what he's done to me.

'Nick.'

There, I can hear a voice saying my name. My father's calling me, but I don't want to hear. I'm not interested in a single thing he has to say to me. I've had enough of his lies. Enough of the smooth exterior and the mass of treachery rushing below.

He's calling to me, telling me to stop. He wants to explain. He's going to make everything better. Because that's what he does. He's the fixer, the righter of wrongs. Yes, that's my father, always shaking somebody's hand, looking into somebody's problem. I can remember sitting in the front row of his meetings, gazing up at him. He was always so strong, so assured, so sure of himself. He was the same on TV, fielding questions with ease, the man of action, the decision-maker.

And the blood won't stop.

'You broke my nose, you scumbag!'

It's the same thing over and over again. I'm backing away, appalled by the blood.

'Nick, you've got to listen to me.'

'No,' I'm yelling. 'No, I really don't.'

That's when I see the car keys. They're on the hall table next to the pegs where we hang our coats, the big plastic tray where the wellingtons go. I make a grab for them. I see his eyes wild with panic.

'Nick, put them down. Please give me the keys.'

I'm not listening. There's nothing he can say that's going to make a blind bit of difference.

'Nick! Come back.'

I'm out of the door and running for the car. My trainers pound on the newly laid block paving. The work is almost complete. There's a small section to the right of the spot where my father parked the Beemer earlier. It's waiting to be finished. My hands are tearing at the door handle. There's the thud, thud, thud as I tug at it before the lock's had time to release. I've got to get inside before he catches up. It takes three goes, but I tug it open. I lock myself in and start the engine. He's outside, face pinched and pale against the darkness.

'Nick, don't be stupid!'

I have an answer for him. 'Don't tell me what to do. Don't even try. You don't have the right!'

He starts pounding on the door, hammering at the window. He's struggling to control his voice. At last, my father manages a semblance of composure. That's familiar. I've seen him do this when an interviewer has him on the rack. Maybe it goes back to his military training. Deep inside, he is pleading with me to see sense, to open the car door and hand him the keys. He's talking slowly, with almost unnatural deliberation and control, trying to hide the fact that he's afraid.

'Listen, son, just turn off the engine and give me the keys.'

I bawl at him to leave me alone.

'You're in no state to drive. Come on, Nicky, just get out of the car. You've got to give me a hearing. It's not the way it seems.'

Well, you got that right. Nothing's the way it seems. Everything's a lie.

'Calm down, son. Let's talk.'

He moves round to the front of the car, peering through the windscreen. For all the rationality in his voice, his eyes are desperate, like a starving man staring through a window at a feast.

'There's nothing to talk about. There's nothing you can say that's going to change my mind.'

Then I'm acting on impulse. There's no conscious decision as I press the accelerator, just instinct. The engine roars.

'Get out of the way.'

Even now, he thinks he can handle the situation. If he can just find the right words, everything will be all right. He's edging back round. It's like those movies where the cop talks the jumper out of throwing himself off the building, only this jumper's not listening. My father reaches the side of the vehicle, expecting me to kill the engine. I know what he's thinking. The crisis has passed. I'm going to step out sheepishly and stand there, head down, waiting for his words of wisdom. That's the way it's always been.

'Just take your foot off the accelerator.' The engine starts to idle. 'That's it. Let's go back indoors. I'll explain.'

He thinks he's won. Blind rage kicks in and I give him the shock of his life, stamping on the accelerator and sending the car racing forward. I glimpse the sudden blur as he leaps back and stumbles into the bushes. Now I'm careering away from the house. The tyres struggle for purchase on the unfinished paving. I've never driven this fast in my life. Before I know it, I'm surging away towards the main road, gunning along the twisting lane.

The world is coming at me, the black, clutching mass of darkness shrieking through the windscreen. The Beemer is racing out of control. The world is rushing, roaring. The headlight beams slice and stab at the night. My hands are trembling and clammy. The steering wheel keeps slipping out of my grasp.

Christ. Oh, Christ, no!

How long does it take – three, five seconds – before I slam into the oak? Shadows lurch into view. Time ceases to have any meaning. In those few brief seconds I take it all in, the hiss of the tyres, the bits of surface spitting into the undergrowth to either side of me, a sound like gunfire, the skeletal branches clawing at the dark. I'm screaming. A split second later I hit the tree.

I don't remember any more.

■

It was the blood.

I ran because of the blood. It was the blood that sent me hurtling into the tree, the blood that put me in this hospital bed. Seeing my father standing in front of me, his arm round Saffi's thin shoulders, reassuring her, it's hard to associate him with the blood. He's dressed in black trousers, brown leather boots buffed to a shine, check shirt, angora sweater hung casually over his shoulders, sleeves looped loosely over his chest.

He's no stranger to blood.

He saw blood.

He saw people die.

That is a soldier's life. He led his men into action. They killed and they were killed. He had to look into the dead eyes of a young man who had fallen serving his country. He had to imagine grieving parents, brothers, sisters, sweethearts, wives, children. He had to begin to frame the words that would confirm their worst nightmares.

That does something to you.

He's staring at me, wondering if I will ever come

back to life. There are so many messages in those eyes and I can only decipher pain and fear. But why fear? What is he afraid of? For all the suspicion, all the dread that is evident in his look, I know he wants me back. But for now, I'm where I want to be, trapped in my useless, crushed body.

Oh, I'd give anything to walk again. I'd love to climb the hills, crash into a tackle, swim. I miss Maria. Especially I miss Maria. I want to touch her hair, press my lips to her face. But here I am beyond pain. Nothing can touch me. Nobody can reach me. As soon as I live the pain will start. No, I'm content to sit here, thank you very much, a kaleidoscope of splintered thoughts, a lost soul swimming in a haze of numbness. It's better than what I had before.

Grandad's talking now. 'Has he moved at all?'

Mum's voice. 'No.'

'What, nothing? Not even the blink of an eye?'

'Nothing. He's been like that since they brought him in.'

Saffi turns round and presses her face into my father's chest.

'He scares me.'

Mum misunderstands. 'We're all worried about him, darling, but he will get better.'

Saffi starts shaking her head.

'No, I mean *he* frightens me. Don't you see the look in his eyes? He's angry about something.'

Mum's stroking her hair.

'Nick isn't angry, poppet. We're not even sure he can hear us.'

Saffi isn't about to make any concessions. 'He can hear.'

'Saffi . . .'

'He knows everything we're saying. There's something in his eyes, Mum, something bad.'

There's something in my father's eyes too.

'Don't, Saffi darling, you're imagining it.'

'I am not! Why are you saying that? Nick can hear everything we say. His brain is as sharp as it ever was. Can't you tell?'

Saffi's got everyone staring at me. She fumes at the blank looks.

'Just look at him! I tell you, he's angry about something.'

Now everybody's trying to comfort her. I watch them crowding round the only one in the room who has the faintest idea what's going on. Maybe it takes a sister to know the truth. Before long, the moment passes. For a while, I slip into the background. They talk about other things. Mum's showering Saffi with attention.

Saffi smiles.

'Don't worry, Mum. Grandma and Grandad are taking care of me just fine. I like it at their house.'

Grandma laughs. 'She likes the dogs, she means. She's been walking their legs off since she came to stay.'

Mum gives my grandparents an uncertain glance.

'I wouldn't mind having a talk before you go,' she says. 'You know, sort out arrangements for the rest of the week. To be honest, I'm in bits. I don't know where I am most of the time.'

Grandma lays a hand on her arm.

'Olivia, it's quite understandable. We're here for you.'

Mum smiles.

'You've both been very good.'

'Why don't you all go to the café?' Saffi suggests. 'You too, Dad. I'll be fine sitting with Nick.'

I watch her face. What gives, Saff? Since when did you start wanting me all to yourself? She wants to talk, only not with the adults around. What's on your mind, little sister?

'I could do with a break,' Mum says. 'Do you mind, Saffi love?'

'Of course not.'

By now, she's almost shooing them out of the door. Don't lay it on too thick, Saff. You've got me curious.

'She's a sensible girl, our Saffi,' Grandad says. 'Come on, let's get that cup of tea.'

I listen to them go. Saffi's face is turned away from me as she watches the door close.

'Listen to them, Nick. You'd think it was all happy families, wouldn't you? You should hear what Grandma says about Mum behind her back.'

I can imagine. There's never been much love lost between them. My grandparents have never thought Mum was good enough for their son.

'I wish they wouldn't talk about her in front of me. She's my mum.'

Saffi pauses. Her gaze is on me now, firm, steady, intelligent.

'You've got something on your mind, Nick. I know it. I'm sure Dad's hiding something. He's all, I don't know, *shaky*.' She frowns, knowing there must be a better word for it, but I get what she means. 'You're not crazy like some boys, Nick. You wouldn't just jump in his car for nothing. Why would you do that? What happened?'

Very impressive, little sister. You've just realised what nobody else has. I've got something on my mind all right. There's just one problem. It's no more than a few fragments, shards of fallout that tear my flesh and slash my mind. From time to time they start to knit together. Then there's a man kneeling in a room, blood gushing from his nose. There's a speeding car and a distant secret fluttering through darkened halls. And all the while dead eyes blaze through the gloom. Saffi brings me back.

'What's it all about, Nick? You could be in a wheelchair for the rest of your life.' Her voice trembles. 'You wouldn't put yourself in danger for nothing. I know you're a pain sometimes, but you're my big brother. I want you back.'

I watch the tears run down her cheeks.

'Whatever made you do it?' she sobs, gulping hard to stifle the sound. 'It's got to be something really bad.'

My little sister's growing up. She's developing a sixth sense. There's a dark shadow on her and she can feel its chill.

'I can't believe Dad would do something wrong. I can't.' Her palm covers her mouth. 'I'm scared, Nick.'

She rubs her tears away and stares at her hands.

'I want my life back. We were happy, weren't we? So what happened? What made you do it?'

She's picking at the bedding, her hair falling forward over her face.

Then there are six of us in the room. That's how hours pass here. My mind shuts down and I'm in another time. I watch people intently. They're all dressed the same. Right, it's the same evening, only later. Mum puts her arm round Saffi's shoulder.

'Have you been talking to him, Saffi? The doctors say that will help.'

She glances at my father.

'We can take turns. We can remind him of the happy times we had. He's coming back to us. He's got to.'

Grandad looks uncomfortable and grunts something. It sounds like *chin up*. Ah great, now I'm part of a war film. He consults his watch.

'I think we'd better make a move, Tim. Saffi's got to be up early for school.'

My father nods and touches Mum's arm.

'What about you, Olivia?'

She rests her cheek against him then she pulls away.

'I'll stay.'

My father thinks about arguing, but confines himself to discussing small details. He's noticed her coldness, same way I did. He gives her a set of keys.

'We're down to the one vehicle until I pick up the courtesy car. I'll get a taxi.'

They're falling over each other to be the perfect couple, considerate, loving, together.

'No,' Mum says. 'You can take mine.'

My father insists. 'You don't know what time you'll be coming home, Olivia. I'll feel happier if you have the car.'

Mum smiles. It's been a while. 'You're far too protective. Taxi drivers are perfectly safe and reliable, you know.'

'All the same. You take the keys. I'll get a cab.'

I listen to the conversation. There's none of the intimacy I heard yesterday. It's like a game of chess. Each piece they move represents an emotion stifled, a thought carefully processed and managed.

'What did the garage say about your car?'

'It's a write-off. They asked about Nick. The

manager seemed surprised at the extent of his injuries.'

'Of course he did. The company doesn't want anybody asking questions about the vehicle's safety.'

'Safety isn't an issue here, Olivia. We can't shift responsibility for what happened. Nick's the one who was driving without a seatbelt. He's the one who ploughed the car into a tree.'

I sense the tension rising again.

'You don't need to remind me.' She drops her gaze. 'The night of the accident, didn't Nick say anything, anything at all? Why would a sensible boy set off like a racing driver? It doesn't make any sense. He must have said something.'

I watch my father's long, slow shake of the head.

'Everything was normal, Olivia. There's nothing to tell.'

'You're quite sure? Nothing happened?'

He's slick.

'Nothing.'

And a word punches into my mind.

Liar.

■

It's the same routine as yesterday.

Mum clamps a pair of headphones to my ears. I recognise the sequence of music instantly. It's my playlist. There's hip hop, indy, R&B, some rock standards from the distant past. Mum's determined to follow through on this therapy course of hers. She's so earnest, I feel like smiling. But I can't. My face is a mask.

At least my mind is active. The human brain must be like a computer. It's searching for a signal. Things are starting to slot into place, whether I want them to or not. So this is the status for Nick Mallory. I'm in hospital, being tormented by my mother. She's Torquemada and her torture instrument of choice is the playlist.

'Listen to this one, Nick. It's your favourite.'

Paloma Faith's smoky voice fills my head. 'Only Love Can Hurt Like This'. Love didn't hurt at all when I chose this one. I'd met Maria. Love was joy. Love was the highlights in her eyes, her perfume filling my senses. Paloma hits the high notes and it's at least two notches too loud. Only volume can hurt like this, but I can't complain. I can't grimace or shake my head. I can't raise my voice in protest or rip the stupid headphones off.

Maybe Mum wants me to start hurting. She wants me to feel the throb of bones knitting, the grind of flesh mending. She wants me to suffer the tide of memory. Well, I'm not ready to remember every gory detail of what happened. I've got me. I've got her and Saffi and my father. I've got Maria, or I will have when she comes to visit me. Yes, and I've got the man with the dead eyes screaming at me from the bottom of the bed.

A strange peace has begun to assert itself, a kind of nirvana. I know nothing of the world's pain. There's the retreating sunlight and the boom of the depths in which I'm suspended. I don't want the world above. I don't want memory getting its claws into me. I don't want explanations and reality and responsibility.

But Mum's like a lifeguard ploughing through the waves in her orange swimsuit, hauling me out, demanding I open my eyes so the sun can burn them. She wants to pump my chest. She wants me to spew water and splutter and stare into the eyes of the thing that threw me here in the first place.

I'm angry with my father, but I wish Mum would just get out of the room, climb in her car and let me glide through the deep water. I want my world of non-pain and non-memory.

I want oblivion.

Through Paloma's final cry of anguish, I hear my father's voice echoing through the house the night I fled.

'Don't run!'

The words have no effect. I'm running, running from the fierce whipcrack of his voice. No, even that's a lie.

I'm running from myself. Mum makes sure I don't get far. She's made it her mission to drag me back into the world of the living, the knowing. Her voice is soft, but insistent.

'I know you can hear me, Nick.'

Of course I can hear you. You don't give me any choice in the matter. I mean, enough already. I get it. You love me. Only love isn't a pillow you shove down on somebody's face. You're choking me, Mum. You're choking me.

'Don't be afraid. You will come back to us.'

That's precisely what I'm afraid of. Why would I want to come back into the glare of knowledge? This betrayal, this hidden sin of my father, is no more than a shadow right now. I don't want to look upon its face. I can't.

Mum is unaware of my thoughts.

'This was taken when your dad left the Forces. Do you remember?'

Yes, Mum, I remember.

'You must have been eight or maybe just nine. Saffi was five. It was wonderful to have your dad home for good. All those years he was soldiering, I never really understood what he was going through. Oh, he told me about all those places: Northern Ireland, Sierra Leone, Iraq, Afghanistan, but that's all they were, Nick, places, pins in a map.

'How does a wife understand what her man is going through? I had this normal, everyday life. But what was his idea of normal? I didn't have to walk with him along some rain-swept street in Belfast or

Derry and dodge bricks and petrol bombs. I didn't have to trudge along some wadi in Afghanistan, wondering whether my next step would be on an IED.

He told me once that he saw a group of kids playing on the edge of town. His patrol was making its way along a line of mulberry trees when he saw a man break cover. He was acting suspiciously. Your dad saw the children getting closer and that's when he realised what was happening. The guy was in the Taliban and he had just planted a mine. Your dad started shouting to the kids not to come any closer. It was too late. Two of them were killed. The villagers blamed him and his men because he was there when it happened. He had to stand there while the kids' mothers screamed at him.'

She paused and I imagined it with her. I thought about Helmand, the backstreets of Iraq with its steel gates, explosives and endless hooded, hostile eyes, the African bush with its unpredictable militias. When I snap back, Mum is still talking.

'We were all sitting in the garden. Oh, it was so lovely. You said it was like a picnic. We had sandwiches and sausage rolls and I cooked my lemon drizzle cake. Do you remember how much you loved my lemon drizzle cake? You used to help me with it and I'd let you lick the mix from the bowl.'

I remember. My father was very quiet the

afternoon he got home. It was as if he was still out there in the war zones. Mum used to say that he was haunted by what he'd seen.

'It was such a beautiful summer. The evenings were long and we sat together talking. Saffi kept trying to do handstands and falling down in a heap.'

Was it really that idyllic? Her words conjure a different picture in my mind. Saffi and I were either side of Mum. My father was sitting apart, chin propped on his cupped hands. He gazed out across the rolling parkland at the back of the old house. I was only a kid, but even so I knew he wasn't happy. I guess part of him wanted to be back in uniform where he knew his place.

'That's when your grandad came up with his master plan,' Mum continues. 'Do you remember? Your dad took for ever to tell me. He thought I would make fun of him. That wasn't far off the mark. I actually burst out laughing when he said he was going into politics. He had never shown the remotest interest in it. He's a man of action, not ideas.'

She is smiling as she speaks. I think she is almost unaware of my presence. She is back there, on the patio, gazing out across the fields and woods.

'Poor Tim,' she says, a smile playing on her lips, 'I don't think he really wanted to do it, but he was always Daddy's boy. There was never any question about his allegiance. It's a tribal thing. Did you know he wanted to go into medicine, but your grandad wouldn't have it? He banged on about Dad going into the Army, until he gave in and signed up. Mallory Senior is a forceful individual. I think he's living his dreams through Dad.'

Now she's looking at me.

'I hope we never put you under that kind of pressure, Nick. You need to make your own choices in life. I don't want to be some pushy mum driving my poor boy to distraction. Do you know what Dad said?'

No, Mum, enlighten me.

'"Lonely nights in a Forward Operating Base give you plenty of time to think." Then he said something that shook me: "Death was all around me. I thought about life."'

Well, what do you know, my father could be a bit of a philosopher. Can't say I've ever seen that side of him.

Life and death, eh? Way to cheer me up, Mummy dearest. She picks up the tale, interrupting my thoughts.

'The sitting MP was thinking of standing down,' she says, 'though I think the constituency party was giving him a bit of a push myself. There were issues.'

She holds up an invisible glass and does the glug, glug thing.

'They thought he should spend more time with his family.'

46

She watches me for a while, as if expecting a response, then resumes.

'There were rumours about his expenses too. Your dad was the perfect candidate: military background, local connections, high profile. He was young, handsome, charismatic, a born leader. He used to show you how to march and drill. Do you remember that?'

I remember.

'You loved it. You were like Dad's shadow that summer. You trotted round after him like an adoring puppy. You even asked if you could follow him into Parliament. Before we knew it, it was a done deal. Tim Mallory was on the road to Westminster. He was an easy sell, of course. Everybody likes a war hero.'

She had said something like that while we sat out on the porch that day. I remember beaming. What nine-year-old boy doesn't want their father to be a hero? Mum's words had my heart beating fast. But right now, lying in my hospital bed, the word is stained with blood. A dark, echoing house is calling me, demanding I take another look at the hero.

MARIA

Maria looks good. Her hair is loose. I wait for a smile, an embrace, but I wait in vain. There's something about the way she enters the room, slowly, hesitantly, gaze flicking right and left. She half turns and glances over her shoulder.

I've been waiting for her visit. I've been building it up like some beautiful glass pyramid and it has just shattered in front of me.

OK, her face was never going to light up. What she's got in front of her is a monster, spewing tubes and drips. I didn't expect hearts and flowers, but you'd think she could manage a smile. Just a little one. Suddenly, I've got panic clawing at my insides. I feel as if I've swallowed razor blades. Is it something I've done? Is that why she's stayed away so long?

She takes a step forward, two, examines the IV, the monitor and finally, the motionless form on the bed. Me. Her hand moves to her mouth. Her eyes don't stay on me long. So what's she thinking? She seems troubled. This is more than disappointment. It's devastation. Maria's visit was going to be a highlight. She was a promise, a hazy, soft-focus dream, but the expected joy has burned away. She still hasn't made eye contact, not really. I was afraid of the man with the dead eyes. Now I'm even more afraid.

At that moment, Nurse Choudhury appears. 'Oh, I didn't realise Nick had a visitor. Are you a friend of his?'

Maria nods her head absently. 'Yes, something like that.'

Something like that! Now I'm *something*. What are you saying, Maria? You're my girlfriend ... aren't you? Isn't that right? It feels right. The idea fits like a hand in a glove. There's an image of the two of us in my head. We're larking about, play-fighting as we make our way down the potholed lane to my house. Her gaze continues to wander, distracted, unsettled.

'I'll come back, Miss ... ?'

Maria hears the implicit question and answers in

a voice that is little more than a whisper.

'I'm Maria, Maria Barnes.'

'I'm Nurse Choudhury.' There's that winning smile again. 'Call me Anita.'

'Nice to meet you . . . Anita.' Again, Maria looks a little embarrassed, lost for words. 'Is Nick . . . I mean . . . Can he hear me?'

Nurse Choudhury, Anita, is keen to deliver good news.

'So the doctors say. Tests suggest that he is alert. There's no physical obstacle to him making a full recovery.'

That is an interesting turn of phrase. There's no *physical* obstacle. So I'm losing my mind, is that what they're saying? She leans forward, whispering a conspiratorial message.

'I'm no expert, you understand, but I can see the intelligence in Nick's eyes. He knows what people are saying to him.'

At least Maria is asking after me. I thought at first she was going to bolt out of the room in panic.

'Is he in pain?' she asks. 'Is he suffering?'

Even now, she doesn't use my name. She's saying all the right things, but there's no warmth in her voice. I had this image of her visit, a perfect moment. When everything else seemed maggoty and rotten, Maria represented something good and wholesome. I would be healed. Now, with every passing minute, her behaviour is picking away at that perfection, pulling open the seam to reveal something I don't want to see.

What did I do wrong?

As soon as I ask the question, there's a new doubt. Can it be true? Did I do something to change the way she felt about me? I want to find this person I've christened Past Me and subject him to interrogation. What did you do, you fool? What the hell did you do to foul things up?

Nurse Choudhury touches Maria's arm lightly. 'I can come back later.'

'No, that's all right. Do what you have to.'

'Are you sure?'

I'm pleading silently for Maria to let her go. Why can't she sit beside me the way Mum does, take my hand even though I won't be able to feel her touch, just be my friend, not somebody who is halfway to being a stranger?

Forget what Past Me did, I plead. This is Present Me, Future Me, the only me that matters. I need *you*. At last Maria takes a seat and looks on while Nurse Choudhury takes my blood pressure and checks the IV and monitor. She tears a sealed pack.

'What's that?'

'Mouthwash.'

She rubs away with gauze on a stick. There's a vague sensation of pressure, possibly the first sign of feeling I've experienced. It reminds me of the dull pressure you feel when you have a filling. She's using a pink solution. I'm glad I can't taste it. Nurse Choudhury is close. She fills my field of vision, blocking my view of Maria.

'I've got a son Nick's age,' she says.

This is a surprise. Nurse Choudhury doesn't look old enough to have a teenage son. There's no comment from Maria. I don't remember when I've seen anybody looking more ill at ease. Not for the first time, she glances at the door.

'There,' Nurse Choudhury says, binning the pack and the disposable gloves. 'All done. Oh, here's Nick's mum.'

Maria looks crestfallen. She was looking for an escape route when Mum turned up. What's going on? I mean, we were perfect together. Those pictures I have in my head, they can't possibly be wrong. I'm right, aren't I? I feel crushed. Past Me must have really screwed things up. This isn't the way a girlfriend reacts.

'Maria! So thoughtful of you to visit Nick.'

Am I imagining it, or is there a mismatch between her words and her tone of voice?

'It's the least I could do,' Maria says.

Listen to her. She is definitely uncomfortable. I see the same squirm of unease, the same furtive glance at the door.

'Have you been here long?' Mum asks.

Maria shifts her feet.

'No, not long,' she answers.

There is a tense silence. What is this? That's when Mum asks her question, the thing that's been nagging away at her.

'Nick usually walks you home when you visit, but not the night of the accident. Why was that?'

'Mrs Mallory, this isn't the time . . .'

'Isn't it? You were at the house, but you weren't in the car with Nick. What happened in that interval?'

It's Nurse Choudhury's turn to look uncomfortable.

'Maria?' Mum says. 'Did you two quarrel?'

'It wasn't like that,' Maria replies.

'So what was it like?' Mum's eyes are fierce. 'I think it's time you levelled with me.'

Nurse Choudhury interrupts politely.

'Maybe Maria's right,' she says. 'I don't think it's such a good idea to discuss this in front of Nick. We don't want him getting agitated.'

Maria seizes the opportunity.

'I've got to go,' she says apologetically. 'There's a thing. At school.'

Oh, a *thing*. What kind of thing? Then my anger is dissolving. Don't go. Talk to me. Please, Maria. Whatever I did, however I hurt you, I'll put it right. I promise.

'Well, it was good of you to come,' Mum says icily.

I want to scream. It wasn't meant to be like this. Maria vanishes from view. The draught excluder hisses as she leaves. I'm yelling inside, pleading with her not to go. Please, Maria, come back. Look at me the way you used to. I'd been looking forward to her visit more than anything and now all I've got is Mum and her photos.

Oh great, she's brought her laptop. Mum's homemade therapy has just gone digital. She flips the machine open. Oh, whoopee. She's got a slideshow for me to watch! Why doesn't she go the whole hog and project a PowerPoint on the wall? Yes, invite the whole hospital round for drinks and canapés while you show them Nick Mallory's greatest hits.

Slide one: Nick in nappies.

Slide two: Nick starting to walk.

Slide three: Nick thinking he's got a girlfriend.

Slide four: Nick having a sixty-mile-an-hour face-off with a tree.

Slide five: Look, it's Lego Nick, in little plastic bricks.

The slideshow starts to play. I would look away if I could. What's happened to make Maria act like that? Mum's running commentary breaks in on my thoughts.

'Look, Nicky. We had so many happy times. We've always had such lovely family holidays.'

Stop, Mum. Please stop. You're trying way too hard. You're reinventing the past, retouching it so there are no blemishes. Everything is just too perfect, too fun, fun, fun. She doesn't listen.

'Look, this is us at Disney World. You loved Florida. Do you remember the villa? Remember how your dad used to take you out on that jet-ski.'

For a moment, I do remember. He let me drive so I did a sharp turn and threw him off into the warm sea. It took him for ever to hoist himself back into the seat. I was howling with laughter as he flopped around like a seal. Later, he took over the controls and it was my turn to be hurled into the ocean and there was his hand, strong, reliable, reassuring, reaching down out of the sunlight. Things were different then. We were father and son and we were tight.

'We could go back this summer. You'd like that, wouldn't you?'

Of course I would. Life was simple then. Every day was an adventure, but there was no danger, no uncertainty. My parents kept me safe. They were gods and I was happy. But I'm seventeen, not six. I'm past rushing into the kitchen to open the window on my advent calendar. I'm past making a diary and crossing off the days until the summer holidays. But I have to sit through every shot, me with Mickey, me on Space Mountain. Then it's a later visit and the family has grown so it's Saffi and me with Mickey, Saffi and me on Space Mountain.

The pictures keep coming: Universal Studios, the Everglades, the Grand Canyon. It isn't just the States either. There's Paris, Amsterdam, Mauritius, Hong Kong, Australia.

'We can visit all these wonderful places just as soon as you get better. Please, Nicky, just give me a little sign that you can hear me. Anything.' Tears are welling in her eyes. 'You will come back. Your dad and I love you so much.'

She isn't even looking at the slideshow. One picture morphs into another. And then, quite unexpectedly, there's a photo that starts a shock running through me.

It's a stocky, balding man with a neatly trimmed goatee beard. He's sitting at the wheel of a Barracuda yacht. I can see the name on the hull.

My father and I are leaning through the window of the cabin. We're wearing matching white polo shirts and identical, suntanned smiles. It's seven years ago. I'm nine years old, nearly ten. There's no tension between us here. The panels arrange themselves and the photo slides off the screen.

We are back to Disney, Universal Studios, Mauritius, happy families, gift shops and sun. I wait for the shot of the man in the yacht to return, but Mum shuts the lid of the laptop with a sigh and I'm left with my questions and a whole lot of misery. The image of the bald man splinters into fragments of light dancing on the ocean and I'm back to worrying about Maria.

■

Later, maybe the next day or the one after that, Saffi is sitting with me. She's giving Mum a break. My father is nowhere to be seen.

'Mum says Maria came.'

Yes, and what a success that was. Saffi reminds me of the first time I saw Maria Barnes.

'I never told you this, Nick, but I've always thought you and Maria were great together.'

I have an image of that first meeting. It was early spring, I think.

'Do you remember, Nick. The deputy head, Mr McLellan, was showing us round when a bunch of girls jogged down the steps outside the library.'

I try to picture Mr McLellan, but his face is elusive. Saffi continues:

'One of them was Maria. You should have seen your face. It was as if you'd been struck by lightning. I nearly burst out laughing.'

Yes, yes, that's right. I see the sixth form girls. They were dressed in the same navy blue school sweaters and tartan skirts, but I only had eyes for one. The wind caught Maria's sleek, straight, black hair and it lifted, showing the lines of her throat, chin and cheekbones.

'Maria noticed you too. She said something to

her friends. They all started laughing then they hurried off to class. You were in another world, Nick. Mr McLellan had to clear his throat to get your attention. You saw me looking at you and you went red. We followed him to the office. Mum was filling in our forms. You'd been grumbling about moving schools, but the sight of Maria stopped your protests dead. Oh, I saw you, big brother. I can read you like a book.'

Really, Saffi? Well, maybe it's true, but where's your sixth sense about our father?

'I was there the first time you talked to Maria,' Saffi continues. 'It was a horrible day. It was April, but it felt more like winter. The week before had been warm. There was blossom, but the wind had blown it over the ground. The rain was turning it to mush. Mum dropped us off, do you remember? She was in a hurry and there was a line of cars crawling into school.'

I watch Saffi's face as she talks. She's bright, my sister, and what a memory! 'There was a smile and a wink for you and a kiss for me. Honestly, she still treats me like a little girl. I headed for the main building, thinking you were just behind me, but you'd spotted Maria arriving. I stopped to see where you were. Maria had just got out of the car and her mum was shouting.'

That's right. Yes, that's right, Saffi. I can see it now. The gunmetal sky darkened and the wind roared. Cold rain swept across the school campus in glittering sheets. Maria started to run. I caught up with her and raised my jacket over her head. My heart was pounding. It was the most perfect moment of my life.

'Going my way?' I asked.

She shouted against the howl of the wind.

'If that's inside, you're on.'

QUESTIONS TO ANSWER

Mum has her arms folded. My father shifts his feet, flicks a glance her way, messes with his hair. The wind is pawing at the window like a dog that wants to come in.

'Just try, Tim,' she's saying. 'Talk to him. We need to stimulate his memory.'

I lie there, wondering what my father is meant to do. She's been monopolising the Tardis.

'I don't know how, Olivia. You're better at this than me.'

Mum's lips pinch with frustration.

'Don't you dare, Tim. That's your son lying on that bed, your only son. The doctors say Nick

60

needs to hear our voices. Talking to him is all part of bringing him back.'

'It's just . . .'

'It's just *what*?'

'I'm no good at this touchy-feely stuff.'

Aren't you? You talked to those men recuperating at Headley Court. Why am I so different?

'Seriously, Olivia,' he says, 'do you think it works?'

Mum isn't letting go.

'Do you know it doesn't? Surely we have to try everything. I don't understand what the problem is. You and Nick have always been thick as thieves. What's so difficult about talking to your son?'

Yes, go on. Enlighten me. I want to know. Finally, my father tries to explain. Here he is, the guy who fixes things, spends hours talking to wounded soldiers, helps people with their problems, and he can't or won't do anything for his own son. What happened to you? When did you stop caring?

'I feel so stupid, you know, self-conscious, talking to somebody who just . . .'

'Who just what?'

'Who . . . lies there.'

'Well, there's no need to feel self-conscious,' Mum says. 'He's your son, Tim. He can hear everything you say. I know it. Please talk to him.'

Once she's gone, my father looks down at me. For a long time, he doesn't say a word. He's glancing at the TV screen, fiddling with his phone. Finally, he mutes the TV and shoves his phone in his pocket.

'It wasn't supposed to turn out like this,' he says. 'How did things get so bad?'

I don't know. You tell me. Strangely, he starts talking about himself.

'Everybody says I'm ambitious. It's all about climbing the greasy pole, becoming a junior minister, moving on to high office.' He shakes his head. 'You know what? I didn't want any of it. I've been on a rollercoaster, Nick. I don't feel as if I had any choice.'

I watch him looking around the room.

'They've made me somebody I don't want to be.'

They? I'm guessing he means the party, Grandad.

'Do you know I wanted to be a doctor when I was at school? I could have done it. All my parents had to do was get me a tutor, give me that extra bit of help, but Dad saw me in uniform. I was going to serve my country, make him proud.'

He stands at the window, hands clasped behind him.

'I never had any say. What was good enough for him was good enough for me. It was the same with politics. I didn't choose any of it.' He leans his head against the windowpane. 'Dad made plans. I went along with them. Everybody thinks I'm strong: leader, officer, war hero. No, I'm still a little boy pleasing his daddy. Pathetic, huh? That's why I had to drag you and Saffi along to all those functions.'

He turns round and sits by the side of the bed.

'You think you were the only ones who got bored? I used to wish I could jump in my car, drive away and never look back. I thought about it, you know. I wanted to take you and Saffi and Mum and lounge around on a beach somewhere.' He looks into the distance. 'Me and my stupid dreams.'

No, keep talking. This is the father I remember. It's good to have dreams. Is that what went wrong? Instead of having dreams, you turned into the professional politician. You started saying other people's lines. Oh, you've become good at it, slick, natural, utterly professional, but it isn't you, is it? You're not listening to people's stories any more. You've turned into a machine that goes round pressing palms, making small talk, looking over people's shoulders to see what's next on the itinerary. He lays his palms on the bedside table and groans.

'Do you remember that garden party, Nicky? That was the day they lined me up to be the local MP. I had Councillor Harris pumping my hand and telling me how wonderful it was to have me installed as the prospective parliamentary candidate. Mum hated those events almost as much as you and Saffi did.'

Again, this is news to me. Mum always smiled at everybody, making them feel special. I've never heard her complain once. Councillor Peter Harris was the leader of the council and the most powerful man in the constituency, a calculating grey-haired man in a matching suit.

'Peter never had much of a way with children,' my father says. 'Saffi used to hide whenever he appeared, burying her face in the skirt of Mum's dress.' He hesitates. 'How am I doing, Nicky? Is this the sort of stuff I'm supposed to say?'

Just be honest. For God's sake, say what's in your heart.

He shakes his head. 'Can you even hear me?'

I hear you loud and clear. For a minute back there, I thought you were being sincere. No, you're doing this because Mum told you to. Well, mission accomplished, sir! I just wish you would go and leave me in peace. Fat chance. My father's found something to talk about.

'Peter had all this hair growing out of his ears. You said he looked like Yoda. You were always direct. He asked you what you wanted to be when you grew up. Do you remember what you said?'

No, but I'm sure you're going to tell me. I'm still trying to picture this councillor.

'You said you were going to be a soldier, just like your dad.' His voice fades to a whisper. 'Just like your dad.'

And I said I was proud. I remember that part. Proud of him.

'So that was it,' he continues. 'On a bright summer's day, with my family around me, it was all decided. I would be the party's candidate. It was a safe seat. I would have a job for life.'

A shadow crosses his face.

'For life. That's what I'd agreed to, Nicky, a life sentence.' He's got a wrapper, or a tissue, crushed in his fist. He tosses it in the bin. 'With no remission for good behaviour.'

I can see the people milling around the tombola and cake stalls, dipping in and out of the beer tent. Councillor Harris laid a beefy hand on my father's shoulder. 'You're the perfect candidate, Tim. Take your father's advice and you won't go far wrong. Just don't go shooting your mouth off. Our last MP was a walking grenade. Boom!'

For a while my father stumbles on. I think I must have drifted off. When I surface, he's in honesty mode again.

'Do you remember when you asked Grandad what an MP does? The answer was typical. He didn't talk about working for his constituents. He said an MP tries to become a Minister, maybe even Prime Minister. Eyes on the prize, that's Grandad.'

And I said I wanted to be a soldier just like you. That's when I believed in you.

That was then and this is now. I drift off again, into the deep waters of semi-consciousness where the sounds of the world boom dully. When I emerge, he's thumbing through the messages on his phone.

Mum returns. She sees the furtive way my father slips his phone in his pocket.

'I know you've been making calls,' she says disapprovingly. 'Can't you set aside some time for Nick?'

'I did! I've been talking to him ever since you left.'

The look Mum gives him is full of scepticism.

'It might help if you remind him about all the good times you had together.'

Her words bring me back to that day on the ocean, but the image splinters into bits, leaving only a sense of a paradise lost. My father takes his coffee, adjusts the cardboard collar on the cup.

'I did my best,' he says, 'sorry about the phone. I've got a lot on my plate.'

'And whose fault is that? I never trusted that man.'

There it is again, that man.

'Please don't nag, Olivia. I was new to the game. Maybe I was a bit too keen to make my mark. I honestly thought he was doing something that could save lives. Do you remember when he first contacted me? It was the evening I got back from Headley Court with Nick. Talking to those guys facing a future with prosthetic limbs, I wanted to do something. If there was any way to stop these awful injuries by detecting IEDs, I was bound to jump at it.'

Mum softened. 'That's the problem, Tim. You acted emotionally. Why didn't you look deeper into his background?'

'You know me,' my father said. 'I was impulsive. I thought I was the man to end this horror. I wanted to serve my country, support the guys on the ground. I thought we had a revolutionary piece of kit, something that could be a game changer.'

'You shouldn't have taken it on trust.'

'I know. Olivia, I made a mistake. It wasn't only me. That bloody man hoodwinked everybody.'

Who does he mean?

'I don't know why you had to do it. We didn't need the money.'

My father bridles. 'It wasn't just about the money. I've just explained that. I wanted . . . I wanted to make a difference.'

Mum wrinkles her nose.

'Tim, this latest business, how bad is it?'

'The press is after me. It's going to get nasty.'

'Didn't you have any idea what he was doing? You're not naïve. There must have been signs.'

'How many times do I have to say it, Olivia? He was a professional conman. He hoodwinked whole governments. I wasn't the only one to fall for it.' He shook his head. 'If I could turn back the hands of time, I would.'

'And there's nothing more to tell? There's nothing else that could come back to bite us?'

Suddenly, my father is all reassurance.

'My conscience is clear. It'll blow over then everything will be back on track.'

'What about Nick?' Mum waits for an answer and doesn't get one. 'I'm still getting phone calls from reporters. They've got questions about the accident. They want to know what he was doing driving your car.'

My father reacts angrily. 'They make me sick. They're like vultures. You'd think they could wait until he's better before throwing their dirt around. Well, I won't let them exploit my family just to sell more copies. This is a family matter. It's private.'

'That's what I've been trying to tell them, Tim. They won't take no for an answer.'

His phone alarm goes off.

'That means I've got to go.'

'What time's the interview?'

'6.30 p.m. It's going to be on the regional news.' He sighs. 'Top item. The hounds can smell blood.'

This might be the first time in my life I've ever been interested in the news. Half past six, he said. What time is it now? I can hear a clock ticking, but it's outside my field of vision. My father kisses Mum on the lips and squeezes her arm. He hesitates by the side of my bed then runs his hand over my hair. I don't feel it, of course. I don't feel anything.

The door closes and his footsteps retreat down the corridor, the bass to the treble of the rattling trolleys. It isn't long before Mum has produced her laptop. This time I want to watch. I'm ready to trawl through Orlando and Arizona, France and the Netherlands, Mauritius, Hong Kong and Australia so long as I can get another glimpse of the man steering his yacht. Finally, he makes his appearance. I examine the receding hairline, the slightly greying goatee and double chin.

This isn't the man with the dead eyes. He is a living corpse. This man is completely different, quite fat and very satisfied with himself. So there are two different faces, but both make me equally uncomfortable. The fat man is smiling, sitting with one hand on the wheel, the other clasping a glass of red wine. He's wearing a light blue polo shirt a size too small. His stomach swells against the material. The waistband of his grey jeans doubles over under the weight of his gut. Beyond him, I'm leaning through the window alongside my father. The photo's on the screen for no longer than three seconds. I will have to wait for several minutes before he appears again.

This man's eyes are bright with self-approval. He's smooth, the captain of the ship.

∎

It's 6.30 p.m. I know because Mum was waving her phone about in front of me and I glimpsed the time.

She stepped outside a couple of minutes ago to get something to eat. She tells me all these details. The credits roll at the start of the regional news. There's a picture of my father. Three words are splashed below his face.

Questions to answer?

If I could sit up in expectation, that's precisely what I would do. There are two presenters, a woman in her early thirties and an older man.

'I'm Abbie Thomas,' she says.

Her co-presenter smiles. 'And I'm Mark Dowling.'

It's back to Abbie. 'First up, the MP and the businessman. How much did rising star Tim Mallory know about this man?'

There he is, the man at the wheel of the Barracuda yacht, but he looks far less relaxed in this photo. Here, he's stern-faced and dressed in a pinstriped suit. It looks like a still from an interview conducted outdoors, probably on the steps of a public building.

Just then, Mum returns with a baguette, a bag of crisps and a carton of orange juice. I can smell the salami in the baguette. She sees what I'm watching and mutes the TV. I start yelling inside my head. What did you do that for? A caption rolls across the screen, identifying the man on the yacht. He is Harry Dennis. I'm unable to summon any other details about him.

For several moments I watch, half-crazy with frustration as the presenters take turns to fire questions at my father. He's sitting with his legs crossed, one arm resting on the back of the studio sofa. He's smiling, doing his best to adopt a relaxed posture, but I can read the tension in his face.

I can't make sense of any of it, but one thing is clear, my father is in some kind of trouble. Mum decides even the silenced broadcast is too much for me to see, so she switches the TV off and takes her baguette from the small, brown paper carrier bag. She tears the cellophane wrapper with her teeth and the rich salami smell is even stronger. She takes a bite of the sandwich and chews thoughtfully before mumbling a comment.

'You don't want to watch that nonsense, Nicky,' she says.

She glances at the IV drip. 'I bet you'll be glad when you can get some solid food down you.'

For a second she has distracted me from the business on the TV. Until this moment I haven't thought about food. How long is it since the accident, two days, three, four? It's hard to tell, but surely I should be hungry by now. That I'm not is a reminder that I'm in another place, far from my usual, cosy existence, far from the routine of school, friends and Maria.

Maria.

Why did I have to let her back in my mind?

Where is she now? That's something she and my father have got in common.

Questions to answer.

WHEN DID YOU KNOW?

They're taking it in turns to talk to me now. Everybody has a different style. Mum is focused and sort of intense. She's got these vivid eyes that scorch you like a laser beam. There are times when I wish I could reach out and touch her arm, assure her I'm going to be OK, I don't know, just get her to calm down and be less hyper. In those moments, I feel close to her. All the artificiality falls away and I could listen to her for hours. Then she's Intensity Mum again, trying to stimulate my memory.

She's the best of a bad lot though. My grandparents are hopeless. They belong in some dodgy sitcom on a repeat channel. Grandma just drones on about what a beautiful baby I was. She seems to be trying to turn me into the world's number one expert in baby-gros and bassinets. Until she started her vigils, I thought a bassinet was a dog. As for Grandad, he always runs out of things to say after a few minutes. He talks stiffly and starts to tell me all kinds of stories from when he was young, stuff he's told me a dozen times before.

Then there's my father. It feels completely different with him. There are things he wants to say. I can feel it. At the back of everything, there's this secret, the cause of my fateful drive into darkness. What was so bad that I took off into the night? I know it's got something to do with the fat man on the yacht, but I never get any closer to knowing who he is or what he's done, just this grim, gnawing feeling that I don't trust my father any more.

The door goes. OK, who is it now? Not my grandparents, *please*, not them. They mean well, but they drive me nuts. Soon, I've got a whole new attitude to the next hour. Theo Markham has just perched on the side of the bed. He's still wearing his school uniform. That pretty much tells me the time. He must have come straight from school. Victor Chen appears next. They're my best friends in sixth form. Victor glances over his shoulder.

'This is who you really want to see, Nick,' he says brightly.

I tense with expectation and there she is. Maria

smiles. Well, that's an improvement on last time. It actually looks like she means it.

'We've come a bit mob-handed, I'm afraid,' she says, scooping her skirt as she sits down on the chair nearest me. 'How are you doing, Nick?'

That depends. This new, relaxed Maria bodes well. There's a bit of banter about things going on at school, who's going out with whom, who's broken up with whom.

'It won't be like this for much longer,' Victor says. 'My dad reckons you'll start to feel sensation returning quite soon. He says a lot of it is down to a positive attitude.'

Right, so it was a bad attitude that put me in this hospital bed. Maybe I shouldn't dismiss what Victor says too quickly. His father is a surgeon, but then again how does he know I'm going to recover? It's not as if he's had access to my case notes. I dismiss Victor's reassurances as lame attempts to make me feel better. For maybe twenty minutes they talk at me, to me, over me, around me. Victor suggests a visit to the café.

Theo winks. 'Give the lovebirds some quality time, eh? Do you want anything bringing back?'

'I'll have a coffee,' Maria says, 'and some kind of chocolate biscuit.'

'Coffee and choccy biccies it is,' Theo says. 'Victor's paying.'

Victor gives him a nudge. 'You think?'

'I'll arm wrestle you for it.'

Maria watches them go, goofing around all the way down the corridor and attracting frowns from some of the staff, then gives me a *those guys* look. She's more natural today, easier in herself. That begs a question. Is this good news or bad news? What's making her blow hot and cold like this?

She starts telling me about some minor scandal at school, two of the boarders coming in roaring drunk and trashing some flower beds. I drift away and float on clouds of intoxicated sixth formers and decapitated geraniums. Before long a voice stabs through the numb, echoey landscape of semi-consciousness. A hoarse, tormented voice crackles through the murk.

'When did you know?'

I'm swimming in and out of sleep, floating in the memory-jumble of the fog. Is Maria still there? I hear the question again, louder this time, asked with more urgency. This is a male voice, middle-aged, angry.

'When did you know?'

It's the man with the dead eyes. He's in the room, but this time he's pacing back and forth. Until now, he has always appeared at the bottom of my bed. It's been the same every time. I didn't see him come. I didn't see him go. He was just there. This time he seems oblivious to my presence. He moves restlessly this way and that, shaking his head.

'When, damn you? When did you know?'

The question isn't directed at me. He hasn't even registered my presence. Who's he talking to? His fists fly to his temples. That's when I see it, his mouth yawning open in a silent scream. Simultaneously, a voice surfaces behind me. It's my father. The wall falls away. Behind it, I can see a familiar living room. The blinds are open, revealing the new driveway and the black, silent woods beyond. I'm peering into the night of the crash.

'Pull yourself together, man.'

My father's voice: clipped, military, authoritative. It was directed at the man I know as Dead Eyes. Dead Eyes was bent double, as if suffering from severe stomach ache. He screwed white knuckles into a head weighted down with misery. Just for a moment, I imagined his bony hands burrowing into his own brain.

'I want to know when. You owe me that much.'

'Don't place demands on me. I don't owe you a thing.'

My father's voice is used to talking others out of a crisis, but there was something else, an undercurrent of indifference, even cruelty.

'This has got to stop. Turning up at my surgery is one thing, breaking into my house is quite another.'

Dead Eyes broke in? My mind searches the house. Once again, I'm a camera, but this time my view of the world isn't fixed. I can roam through the various rooms, peek into every recess. I investigate the kitchen. There's no sign of a break-in. It's the same with the front door.

Dead Eyes answered.

'I didn't break in. I didn't have to. For a Member of Parliament, you're not too hot on security, are you, Tim?' His voice is cracked. 'I suppose you thought you didn't have to be. People like you think they're fireproof. Well, think again. All I had to do was walk through the kitchen door and sit myself down. I could have strolled in and trashed the place before you knew I was here. You're lucky I'm not a violent person. Do you want to hear something funny? I even knocked before I entered.'

My father's expression didn't change.

'So you're an intruder with manners. That hardly excuses your actions. You're trespassing on private property. I could do pretty much what I like with you now, you pathetic loser, and not a court in the land would convict me. I would be defending my home and family.'

'Don't give me that. There's nobody here to defend. You're all alone.'

'I would be within my rights if I wanted to evict you forcibly. The law would be on my side.'

Dead Eyes contorted his body then he started to yell.

'Stop changing the subject! This is about something far more important than trespass. I'm going to ask the question again. When did you know?'

My father took a few steps forward before pausing in the middle of the room.

'I will give you one minute to leave this house. If you refuse, I will have no option but to call the police.'

'I thought you were going to throw me out yourself. What's the matter, lost your bottle?'

My father's eyes narrowed.

'Does it really matter? The point is you're going. Yes, I think I will call the police.'

Dead Eyes wasn't impressed. 'That's a bluff. You don't want to call the police.' He tapped his temple. 'Think about it, Tim. You don't want to kick up a fuss. Imagine all those reporters crawling over your property, poking their noses into your affairs. I know too much, you see.'

My father inhaled, pulled his phone from his pocket. 'Is that some kind of threat?'

'It's the truth.'

'You don't know anything.'

I feel as if I'm on the edge of an abyss. The world seems to pitch and tilt. The effect makes me dizzy. Yes, I was at the top of the staircase. When I heard them arguing, I must have started down towards the living room. Then I stopped to listen. There's something else. I wasn't alone. I glanced back over my right shoulder and there was Maria, her face startled and beautiful. I have no memory of how she got there. Her warm breath brushed my cheek for a second. She had to duck down to see my father and his visitor in the living room.

'Who's that man?' she whispered, her fingers closing round my wrist. 'He looks really strange, I don't know, unwell.'

I shook my head. 'I've never seen him before.'

Maria.

Suddenly, it's as if I've summoned her. Time jumps tracks. I'm disoriented. She's in the chair by my hospital bed, sipping coffee from a plastic cup. There's a half-eaten biscuit in her hand. I have a feeling Theo and Victor have gone. Maria glances at her phone.

'Mum will be picking me up soon. Can you hear me, Nick?' She searches my face. 'I hope you can. I've . . . I've been thinking about that night.'

What is she, a mind-reader? She's been thinking about Dead Eyes too. I remember the way he was. He looked ill. His skin was ashen, eyes hollow and ringed with dark shadows.

'I know your parents think I'm to blame . . . for all this.'

That explains Mum's attitude to Maria, but why, what could she have done?

'I didn't mean to run out on you. It's just . . . I'm not used to violence. When your father hit that man . . .'

Her face starts to crumple. I want to take her in my arms, comfort her, but she's unreachable. I can see my father and Dead Eyes quarrelling. Words bounced around the room.

Blood on your hands.

Betrayal.

There are all these faces. Why can't I make sense of them? Maria is talking.

'We were watching on the landing. Do you remember? I was holding my breath, trying not to make a noise. That guy pulled up a chair and sat down, daring your dad to do something about it. He gave me the creeps, Nick. He was unstable. He kept saying the same thing over and over again. He wasn't going to leave the house until he got answers. He even threatened to wait for your mum to get back. I suppose that's what lit the touchpaper, the threat to your family.'

It's as if Dead Eyes is here with us. I can hear him laughing off my father's threat to throw him out. He carried on as if nothing was said. 'How will you tell the children what you've been up to?'

'Keep my family out of it.'

'That's just it, I can't. Nick and Saffron. Nicky and Saffi. You don't hear names like that where I live.'

'Cut it out,' my father warned. 'I would like you to leave.'

Dead Eyes wasn't listening.

'I bet they idolise you, Tim. Can I call you Tim? You can call me Alec. Does Saffi look up to you? Does she worship her famous daddy? Does Nick want to be like you? I can just see him marching in step behind the old man, another officer in the making.'

He snaps to attention. 'Captain Nick Mallory reporting for duty, sah!'

Why's he got to drag me into it?

'I wonder, does your boy fall for all that war hero crap? If only he knew what the real Tim Mallory was like. You see, a true officer will live and die for his guys. He would never do anything that would lead to a man's death.'

'I did my best for the men under my command. Ask anybody.'

'There's somebody I can't ask, isn't there? He's the ghost at this little soiree. I can't ask my son. Now why's that, Tim?'

My father's face was drawn tight. It was as if his skull was expanding outwards. He was becoming as much of a monster as the man who had forced himself into our home.

'When will the family be back, Tim?'

'You keep my wife and children out of this,' my father warned. 'I want you to get out of my house.'

'You'd like that, wouldn't you, Mr High-and-Mighty Mallory, Mr Squeaky Clean, Butter-Wouldn't-Melt-In-His-Mouth war hero? You'd like me to walk away and disappear into the night so that you can carry on with your effortless rise to the top. Well, it isn't going to happen. Everybody's going to know what you did.'

That's when Maria's voice breaks in again.

'I asked you if he was blackmailing your father. Do you remember? You said you didn't know, but I could see the look on your face. Your whole world was falling apart. I know how much you admire your dad.'

Admire him? I did, but not any more. That's why it's so hard.

'Your dad was struggling to stay calm. He didn't know we were listening. He thought we were still out. Oh, Nick, I'll never forget your dad attacking that man. He just snapped.'

Maria flinches visibly as she relives the attack.

'We watched them. Remember the way the chair clattered to the floor? A bowl flew off the table. It was insane. It just exploded out of nowhere. There was so much noise. We watched your dad frog-marching him to the front door. He was twisting and turning, writhing and squirming.'

The memory roars into my mind like an on-coming train.

'Get your . . . hands . . . off me!' Dead Eyes was snarling as he clawed and tore at my father's arm. He demonstrated unexpected strength for somebody so much shorter than my father.

'Get your murdering hands off me!'

He resisted my father with every ounce of defiance he could muster.

'You let go of me and give me some answers.'

By now, my father had succeeded in manhandling him towards the door. Maria gasped and pushed past me. She'd heard what he had said as clearly as I did.

Murdering hands.

'I don't know what the hell is happening here. Nick, I'm scared. I want to go home.'

'Maria, you can't go by yourself. It's dark.'

'Don't worry about me,' she said. 'I'm a big girl.' She kissed me.

Her eyes signalled that she didn't want anything to do with the warring voices in the hall.

'I'll walk you back,' I offered.

I was ready to do anything to escape the madness that had exploded before my eyes.

Maria shook her head. 'No, I don't think that's such a good idea. I'll phone my mum while I walk down the lane. She'll pick me up on the main road.'

'Maria . . .'

She jogged downstairs in her bare feet toward the kitchen door. I remember her skidding briefly on the polished floor in her haste to get away.

The struggle continued a few metres away, oblivious to our presence. My father was trying to get the front door open. He was breathing heavily.

Dead Eyes was causing him more difficulty than he'd expected. He was wiry and had a strength and resilience out of proportion with his scrawny frame. My father's voice echoed through the house, louder, harsher than before. He'd lost control.

'You think you can come into my house and interrogate me about something that happened seven years ago? You think you can blame me for what that crook did? You know nothing about me, you pathetic, miserable clown. All you've got is wild allegations. You'll never make them stick. You have no right to come into my house and throw your unfounded accusations around.'

I saw the white face that was going to haunt me, the eyes that would stare from the bottom of my bed.

'You want to know what gives me the right? My son gives me the right.' Dead Eyes pounded his chest. 'My son!'

There was a scream.

'You broke my nose. You broke my bloody nose!'

My father was leaning into his face.

'I haven't even started. You're going to listen. That man conned me.'

He changed tack, making an attempt to win his tormentor round. Why was he pleading with somebody who had forced his way into our home?

'In a way I'm as much a victim as you are.'

My father's words drew a bitter response. 'Don't make me laugh. A victim. You? You were in cahoots with that scumbag Dennis. He couldn't have done it but for you.' Dead Eyes fixed my father with a look of contempt. 'I've seen that recommendation on his website. You made yourself the acceptable face of his nasty little operation.'

'I gave him that recommendation before I had any idea about his business. I tell you, I didn't know!'

'You knew.' Dead Eyes' voice was a low growl. 'I bet you got well paid for what you did.'

My father got the door open for an instant only for the weight of Alec's resisting body to make it slam again.

'I don't have to listen to this,' he said. 'You're not worth the dirt on my shoes. You're nothing.'

Blood was pouring from Dead Eyes' nose. He was trying to staunch the flow. It made his voice muffled.

'You're right. I'm nothing. Do you know why I'm nothing? It's because you took everything I had. You took my son. You tore my family apart.'

He stabbed a bony finger in my father's face.

'Do you understand? You took my son!'

Something crosses my vision, breaking the spell. It's a moment before I realise. It's Maria's hand. She's stroking my cheek, though I don't feel a thing.

'I didn't mean to run out on you that night,' she says. 'Forgive me, Nick.'

Forgive you? I'd forgive you anything, Maria. Just don't leave me. Please. She sees the time on her phone and rises to her feet.

'I'm going now. I'll come again. Soon.'

I hear her footsteps as she walks away.

Four words follow me into the darkness.

You took my son.

Left alone, I wash around my memories. The same words burst from the depths again and again.

You took my son.

You're a murderer.

The words keep echoing through my mind. The scene I witnessed had the power of an explosion. Filth and debris blast my face. I feel dirty, lacerated. What brought that man into our home? What invited those dead eyes to haunt me? All those accusations he flung at my father, were any of them true? As I lie here trying to make sense of that night, it is like the final hours of darkness before the dawn. The greyness is parting. The sun, still insipid, is threatening to break through. There's nothing kindly about the light of this sun. Dawn will be unforgiving. It will expose everything.

I'm on the verge of knowledge, but I don't want it. Somewhere, deep inside my memory, I know what my father did, but I can't face it. I refuse to face it. I don't want to know what those words mean.

You took my son.

HERO

Well, what do you know?

I got through to another day. It was a quiet night, almost a peaceful one. The man with the dead eyes stayed away. I am very nearly happy, floating in the space between sleeping and waking, but peace is hard to come by when thoughts and suspicions come flying at me like glass from an exploding window.

The door goes. It's the physios. This is the only time I steal a look out of the window. The world shakes as they get to work. There's a seagull standing on a lamppost. In the distance the traffic rushes by. Everybody's got somewhere to go.

The physios flip me over on my left side. This time the only thing I've got to look at is the door. It's about as interesting as . . . well . . . a door. The mauling and thumping starts again. They suction the tracheostomy, the tube that's letting me breathe. They clean the inner tube of the trachy and replace it. It's moments like this when I understand just how helpless I am. They do things to me. I do nothing back.

I am . . . nothing.

Mum turns up soon after the physios finish. She's on the phone to my father.

'What time do you think you'll be home? No, I understand. I'll tell Nick you'll be in to see him tomorrow.'

She seems to register my presence. This time she's got her iPad with her. She flips it open and shows me a photo.

'Do you recognise it, Nicky?'

Kind of. I mean . . . maybe. It's me all right.

'You were seven years old. Look at Saffi. She was so cute in that sun hat. The Army had just decorated Dad for gallantry.'

I feel sorry for that kid. He doesn't know anything about the adult world. I see him there with his nose pressed against the window, watching the giants and wondering why they act the way they do. He doesn't know that great, brave men can carry the seeds of their own destruction. He doesn't know that a story doesn't always end happily ever after.

'They were such good times,' Mum says, scattering my thoughts. 'Why did it all have to get so complicated? Why did he let his father railroad him into politics? I was married to the bravest man in the world. He could have done anything. You were so funny, Nick. One of Dad's men said guys like him ought to run the country. You kept asking when he was going to be Prime Minister. You thought all he had to do was make a phone call and we would be moving in the next day.'

I've got the conversation echoing dully in the back alleys of my mind. The giants danced. They laughed and smiled and exchanged glances and all I could do was wonder at them.

■

My father's back. He has walked in with a word hanging from him.

Murderer.

It came from the lips of the man with dead eyes. It echoed through the house and sent Maria fleeing into the night. My father has just pulled his chair up to the side of the bed while Mum adds two Get Well cards to the growing array on the over-the-bed table. I examine his face.

Murderer.

Can it be true? I know something. I know *something*, but I don't know that he's a murderer.

Other words boom in my ears like liar and traitor, words that planted me in the driver's seat of his car, words that put me in this hospital bed, but the word murderer isn't one of them. It's not part of my splintered vocabulary of emotions. I can imagine this hero becoming many things, but a murderer? I don't want it to be true. It can't be true.

'Any news?' Mum asks.

There's anxiety in her voice. My father doesn't do anything to allay her fears.

'My team are doing their best to field the questions, but we're drowning in them.'

'You'd say something if there was, wouldn't you?'

'Don't you trust me, Olivia?'

'I want to . . .'

Her voice trails off. My father glances in my direction, remembering that I can hear.

'That's hardly a resounding vote of confidence,' he says.

'It's all the questions,' Mum says. 'They get to you. I can't leave the house without some journalist sticking a microphone under my nose.'

My father flaps his hand, as if swatting a fly.

'Ignore them. It'll blow over.'

'Are you sure about that?' she asks. 'There's no sign of the storm blowing itself out yet.'

'They don't have any evidence. Harry Dennis is the guilty party here, nobody else.'

His answer fails to reassure her.

'Harry Dennis is in prison,' she reminds him. 'Tim, if . . .'

'That's right, Olivia,' my father says, cutting her off mid-sentence. 'You got it in one. Harry Dennis is in prison. He's right where he deserves to be. He committed a crime. *He* did.' His voice cracks suddenly and the politician's mask slips. His voice is quieter. 'Look, I'm not excusing myself. I was too trusting, gullible even, but there was nothing intentionally corrupt about what I did. Dennis conned a lot of other people, including Her Majesty's government. I'm just one more victim of his deception.' He took a deep breath and leaned his forehead against hers. 'Please believe me. I made a mistake. But I'm still the same man. I would never do anything to hurt you and the kids. Look, can we change the subject?'

Mum seems happy to drop it, but they seem short of things to discuss. They sit in silence, the only thing uniting them my broken form on the bed.

VISITORS

I have visitors. Mum's here. I can hear my father in the corridor. He's taking a phone call. There's the sound of somebody clearing his throat. That'll be Grandad. He's hovering somewhere out of sight. Presently, the draught excluder makes its whispery buzz on the tiles and Grandma enters with my father by her side.

'We'll have to make a move,' she says. 'Saffi has homework to do and she's up early in the morning.'

'We're going to London,' Saffi explains. 'There's a poetry thing.'

There's tension again. My father's under pressure. I wish I knew what was in that TV news report.

I remember the photo of Harry Dennis, not the beaming, successful man at the wheel of his yacht, but a haunted, pursued figure gazing into the lens of a camera. As he leaned forward, responding to the presenter's close questioning, my father had that same tormented look.

My grandparents finally usher Saffi out of the room a few minutes later. There's a murmur of conversation in the doorway and it dawns on me that there's a new arrival in the room. I tense. It can only be one person.

'Come in, Maria.'

Maria has her hair up and she's wearing a blue dress and dark tights. Her arms are bare and she has her jacket hanging over her right arm. She looks fantastic. Still she doesn't seem that comfortable. What was it Mum said?

You weren't in the car.

Did you quarrel?

Did we? I notice the way Maria tries to position herself as far from Mum as she can.

'Tim and I are going to the restaurant for something to eat,' Mum says.

She means the hospital canteen.

My father pulls a face. 'I wouldn't call it a restaurant.'

'Don't get caught saying that in public,' Mum warns. 'It's not a good idea for an MP to be heard running down the health service, especially when you're thinking of flogging it off to the private sector.'

My father goes to protest at her description of the government's policy, but Mum kills his words with a look.

'We won't be long,' Mum says, ushering my father into the corridor. 'Twenty minutes or so, maybe half an hour.'

Maria forces a smile as she turns to watch them go. For a few moments, her face is lost behind a curtain of sleek, black hair, but when she looks back at me, there's warmth in her expression.

'I'm so sorry, Nick,' she says.

No, don't be sorry. That means there's something to be sorry for.

'I think I've been a bit weird with you,' she says, laying a hand on the bedclothes. 'I shouldn't have let that night freak me out so much. That was all about your dad, not you. It was just so frightening, the way he hit that man, the terrible things they were yelling at each other.'

Is that all it is? It's about the scene in the living room? It's as if she's just read my thoughts.

'There's no need to worry, Nick,' she tells me. 'You're not going to lose me.' Her eyes are intense. 'I'm not that fickle. I thought you knew that.'

She pauses. I watch her examining my face.

'You can hear me, can't you, Nick?'

If I had tears I would cry. Of course I can hear

you, Maria. The memory of your face keeps me company through my darkest moments.

'You've got to come back, Nick.' For a moment she seems to crumple, her chin wobbling, voice thick with emotion. 'I think I might understand. Are you hiding, is that it? Whatever trouble your dad's in, you don't want to face it, do you?'

How can she know this? How can she sit in front of me and understand? Then I have it. She was there. Nick Mallory, you're an idiot. That's it. She told you. She was there in the dark, echoing house that night. She heard all that angry yelling, saw the blood gouting from the intruder's face. She understands because she shares something with me, a sense of the nightmarish shadows creeping around my father.

'I hope I'm not talking nonsense,' she says, giving a twisted, little smile. 'Maria Barnes, psychiatrist.' Her voice trails off then strengthens. 'I don't think so somehow.'

Listen to me, Maria. You're doing just fine. You're the only one who even half-understands. You and Saffi. You're on the right path.

'If there's any truth in it at all,' she says, still gripping my hands, 'if you're afraid or worried, I'm here for you.' Soon she is so close her lips are almost touching my cheek. 'Things happened that night, things your dad isn't telling us. Saffi feels it too and she's a daddy's girl.'

So I'm not the only one who can see through my father.

'I'll be here when you walk out of this place, Nick. I swear it.'

At that moment I want nothing more than to feel her hands. It's so weird, knowing she's touching me, but not feeling the sensation.

'I'm going to be around every step of the way. I was so stupid the other night. Whatever happened between your dad and that man, it's not your fault.'

Isn't it? So why did I run? Why did I grab my father's keys and drive his car away into the night?

'There's nothing to be afraid of, Nick. No matter how bad it is, it can be put right. Nothing's going to scare me away. Trust me.'

At that moment, that marvellous, heart-stopping moment, she leans forward and kisses me. She starts to draw back and that's when it happens. It's as if an electric shock has just fizzed through her, jerking her backwards. What just happened?

'Nick . . . Oh, Nick!'

What? What happened?

'Nick! At last.'

What did I do?

She rushes to the door and peers out into the corridor.

'Nurse! Anyone?'

Then she's back. Her eyes are wide, her face full

of emotions that seem to flutter between joy and amazement. Talk to me. What did I do?

Maria notices a bell on the wall and rings it. Within moments medical staff are crowding into the room. I can see a nurse. It's not Nurse Choudhury. She must be off-duty. There's a doctor too. There may be one or two more.

'When did it happen?'

The doctor is an auburn-haired woman in her late twenties or early thirties, I would guess.

'You're sure?'

Maria nods.

'I know what I saw.'

What the hell was it? What did I do? I'm screaming at them. Tell me!

Soon, Mum is there. My father is behind her, his hands on her shoulders.

'How long ago did it happen?' he asks.

'Just now,' Maria tells him. 'It was so amazing. He blinked.'

I blinked?

I blinked.

How could I not know? Don't you see something when you blink, a shutter coming down, a tiny flicker of darkness? It's such a small thing, a blink, no more than a reflex action. You don't even think about it normally. I have endured despair. I've been trying to make myself a speck of nothingness. Suddenly, Maria gives me something to feel happy about and

I respond. It's the tiniest, most ridiculous thing, but I blinked. To my surprise, Mum practically hugs Maria in her joy at this tiny step forward.

'You got him to listen, Maria. You got him to do something.'

She releases Maria, who looks embarrassed.

'I don't think it was down to me, Olivia.'

'You were here,' Mum says. 'That was enough.'

Now the doctor's the one commanding her interest.

'Does this mean he's on the way back? Doctor, is he going to recover?'

The answer is non-committal, but her tone is positive.

'It's too early to say for sure, but I think this is a good sign, Mrs Mallory. I would definitely say it is encouraging.'

The atmosphere in the room has lifted and all because of the tiniest reflex action.

I blinked.

THE CLEAR BLUE SEA

For an hour after they left, my mind was racing. I expected my thoughts to become lucid and sequenced, my body to rally. As it turned out, nothing changed, nothing at all. My body was stuck in the same rut as my mind. Things improved, became clearer, started to make sense then shuddered into reverse and smashed into bits. The remaking of Nick Mallory was going to be long, confused and frustrating. I lay there without moving and my sense of disappointment was all-consuming.

But I could blink.

Occasionally.

My overblown hopes led to a sleepless night.

Maybe I've managed to convince myself that the damage isn't too bad up to this moment. All I have to do is decide to crawl out from the comfort of not-knowing, not-feeling and I will be back, the old Nick. Now, as I lie here staring at my wall, my TV, the dog-eared poster, the empty foot of the bed, for the first time I am truly afraid.

I blinked. My body threw a switch and the physical world beckoned. That means the pain will start soon. Before long, I will be crawling over broken glass. I can't see any other way back, except through a tunnel of agony. However slowly, however unevenly, sensation will return and with it, long days of suffering as my ruined body tries to rebuild itself. I reel with anxiety at the thought of my knitting bones, my slowly healing flesh.

My memory is in a mess. My recollections are random. They hop. They skip. They jump tracks and career away in every direction, without any rhyme or reason. My thoughts will return to a time when I was thirteen then I am ten, six, four, eleven. No matter how hard I try, I can't seem to slot things into a coherent narrative. It's dark outside. The faulty street lamp buzzes. From time to time a car drones by. Occasionally, a plane grumbles in the dark. Raindrops thud on the skylight. They rap for admittance like lost souls. I've started to wonder about school, the small details of daily life.

All this time, I've inhabited a world cut loose from the moorings of routine and humdrum reality. Now all those dull little details – mealtimes, sports fixtures, lesson timetables, social networking, homework, TV – have started to roam round the edges of my mind. When the mad rush of thoughts subsides, Mum and Saffi are by the bed.

'Look, Mum,' Saffi says. 'He just blinked. Nick's awake.'

'Hi, Nicky.' Some of the weariness has lifted from Mum's face. Just goes to show what a blink can do. 'The doctors are really pleased with your progress. You responded to Maria's voice. That's good. It's really good. Your dad's going to join us later. That will give you something to look forward to.'

'There,' Saffi says, 'he blinked again.'

Yes, I blinked in response to the mention of my father. I focus on Saffi. What does she know? There is a short silence then Mum notices something on the TV.

'Look, Saffi, that's the marina. Remember our boat trip . . .'

She hesitates. That's got my attention. There was a sudden step back. So why did her voice falter so abruptly? What was that about?

'That's right,' Saffi says, unaware of my sudden interest. 'We went out on that yacht. We had a buffet. That was cool, wasn't it, Nick? You loved going out to sea.'

Now she sees it, the same change of expression I noticed.

'What's wrong, Mum?'

She tries to laugh it off.

'Nothing, darling. It's really nothing.'

Saffi continues to frown then Mum manages to guide the conversation away from the boat trip. She's thrown Saffi off the scent, but I'm not that easy to distract. She has evoked a memory. It surfaces like bobbing debris. The fat man was waiting to welcome us aboard his yacht, a Lord-Of-All-I-Survey smile on his lips. He was wearing a skin-tight polo shirt.

'Don't worry, Sonny Jim,' Dennis said. 'I don't bite. I'm Harry Dennis.'

'My name isn't Jim,' I said. 'It's Nick.'

There was laughter. I stared at the sleek lines of the yacht. I had never been on a boat this big or so downright beautiful. I didn't like the fat man, but I decided to give him the benefit of the doubt. Surely nobody who had a vessel this amazing could be all bad?

'OK, My-Name-Is-Nick,' Dennis said, eyes sparkling with mischief, 'how old are you?'

I gave a tight-lipped answer. 'Eleven.'

My father had his arm round my shoulder, crushing me against him. Was he trying to silence me? He was laughing, but his laughter was as exaggerated as Harry Dennis's ridiculous two-cheek kisses. Who did he think he was, the President of France?

'Well, Nick Mallory, aged eleven,' Dennis said. 'What do you think of the boat?'

I stared at the streamlined shape of the Barracuda yacht. I thought it was amazing, but that isn't what I said. I tried to sound casual.

'It's all right.'

That was all he was getting. He had my answer, clipped, surly, snappy, a reminder that I didn't like this man. My snarl of dislike went all but unnoticed. Harry Dennis was one of those men who was so impressed by himself, he couldn't imagine anyone else not being. My father was already in full-on hand-pressing mode.

'A life on the ocean waves, eh?' He ran his admiring gaze along the hull. 'It's magnificent. What did this little baby cost you?'

'Let's say I had to raid the old piggy bank,' Dennis answered chirpily.

My father led the way on board. The marina glittered. There was a faint smell of ozone. It was a perfect day. Before long, the engines throbbed and we carved a path through the calm, gleaming sea. There was another man on board, but I don't remember much about him. Some time after, my father would refer to the guy as a gopher. His job was to go for things. He took the Barracuda's wheel while my father and Dennis put their heads together.

'What are they talking about?' I asked Mum.

'Your dad's got some business with Mr Dennis,' Mum answered. 'He's going to do some consultancy work.'

'What's consultancy?'

'Mr Dennis has got an invention,' she replied.

'Why does he need Dad?'

Mum shrugged and fiddled with Saffi's hat. The sea breeze kept threatening to blow it away.

'It's some kind of military equipment. He wants a soldier's testimony to give it credibility.'

So Dennis needed my father. He needed a hero.

'Can I see it? The invention.'

'I wouldn't interrupt them at the moment,' Mum said. 'Mr Dennis is giving Dad a demonstration.'

For the next few minutes I was kicking my heels, wanting to see Harry Dennis's invention. I imagined a robot soldier, a state-of-the-art machine-gun or a laser cannon. Eventually, my father emerged with Dennis. When I finally got to see the reason for his meeting with Dennis, it came as a big disappointment.

'That's it?'

'This,' Dennis declared, brandishing his invention, 'is it.'

I was looking at what seemed to be a shiny plastic hand-grip with a retractable aerial. It resembled a gun without a barrel.

'What is it?'

I gave him the kind of look that made him burst out laughing.

'This ingenious little piece of kit,' Dennis said, 'is the Sniffer RVX-80.'

I still wasn't impressed. 'It's a plastic gun with an aerial. What does it do? Where do the bullets come out?'

Dennis was in his element. He did a lot of name-dropping, boasting about the various governments that had wined and dined him, the embassies whose rooms he had graced.

'Why don't you give the family a demonstration, Harry?'

Dennis leaned against the deck rails, raising his face to the sun and closing his eyes. 'Would you like one?'

For a reason I couldn't fathom, Mum frowned. 'Is this quite safe?'

I was intrigued.

'Why wouldn't it be safe?' I asked.

Mum was looking at my father. 'It detects explosives. That's right, isn't it?'

'Got it in one, Olivia,' Dennis said, mopping sweat from his neck.

I stared at it. 'How does it detect explosives?'

Dennis ignored me. He was still trying to impress Mum.

'The Sniffer is a long-range molecular locator,' he announced grandly. 'It doesn't just find explosives.

It can also be used in law enforcement – you know, contraband and smuggling. Do you want to see?'

When nobody protested, he invited Saffi over. She clung to Mum, shaking her head.

'What about you, Nick?'

I moved closer, glancing uncertainly at the Sniffer. 'What do I do?'

Dennis had something in his hand that looked like a credit card. 'Has anybody got a pack of cigarettes?'

My father glanced at Mum and shook his head. 'Neither of us smokes.'

Dennis's friend leaned out of the cabin and tossed him a pack. 'Will this do?'

'Perfect,' Dennis said. 'Just put it on the deck over there.'

With the cigarettes placed on the deck a few metres away, Dennis shoved the card in a slot and handed me the Sniffer.

'Hold it like this, Nick,' he told me. 'Off you go.'

'What do I do?' I repeated.

Dennis still had that self-satisfied smile on his face. 'Just walk across the deck. The Sniffer will do the rest.'

I made my way across the deck and the aerial swung suddenly to my left.

'Why did it do that?' I asked, staring in wonder.

'It's a dowsing effect,' Dennis said. 'See, it has located the tobacco.'

'How does it work?'

Dennis's explanation was smooth and confident.

'The user places a small amount of the substance he wants to detect. It could be explosives. In this case it's tobacco. He puts it in a Kilner jar along with one of these stickers. They absorb the traces of the substance.

'The sticker is then placed on one of these cards, which is then scanned by a digital reader and inserted into the device.' He took a sip of his drink. 'That, ladies and gentlemen, is the Sniffer RVX-80. We already have scores of units in operation in the Middle East and Asia. With Tim's recommendation, we will soon be exporting all over the world.'

'Can I have a look?' Mum asked.

Dennis handed it over.

'So this is some kind of card reader?' she said.

'Each card is programmed to identify a different substance,' Dennis answered. 'The Sniffer can be used by drug and smuggling agencies. Our main area of growth is in the detection of explosives.'

Mum returned the Sniffer to Dennis. He stored it in a specially designed briefcase and snapped down the catches. For a moment, his hand rested on my shoulder, leaving a clammy mark on my shirt.

'I'd better put this away,' he said. 'It's an expensive piece of kit.'

He had Mum's attention.

'How expensive?'

'Each unit retails at eight thousand pounds.'

Mum did a double take.

'Eight thousand pounds! Did I hear you right? For each one?'

Dennis didn't blink an eye at her reaction.

'Correct. We discount for bulk purchases. It can bring the price per unit down by fifty per cent, even more if the order is big enough.'

Mum swapped glances with my father.

'And governments are willing to pay that?'

'Land mines and IEDs cost hundreds, thousands of lives in places like Iraq and Afghanistan,' Dennis said. 'Isn't that right, Tim?'

My father nodded gravely. 'I've seen the consequences at first hand. When you've watched a man wade through his own blood on shattered stumps of legs, you . . .'

His voice trailed off. Mum had given him a hard stare to remind him that Saffi and I were listening.

'That's why I'm giving my approval to Harry's device,' my father said, his voice softer. 'It's a simple, hand-held piece of kit, portable and easy to use. This could be to modern warfare what radar was to the Second World War. If it can save lives, it's worth it.'

'All the same,' Mum said, shifting her attention back to Dennis, 'how can you charge eight thousand pounds for something the size of a water pistol? There's nothing to it.'

Dennis had a ready answer. 'There's quite a lot to it, Olivia. Micro-technology is, by definition, small. Our customers are paying for the Research and Development, ease of use and effectiveness.'

Mum didn't look convinced.

'Anyway,' Dennis said, 'lunch is ready.'

Mum still didn't move. She was staring at the briefcase containing the Sniffer.

'You don't look impressed by our product,' Dennis said.

'It's not that,' Mum said. 'I'm just amazed that such a small device can be so effective.'

Dennis chuckled. 'You don't say that about your mobile phone.'

'I beg your pardon?'

'You possess a phone, don't you?'

'Yes, why?'

'It's the size of a pack of cards. Just a few years ago, nobody would have believed mobile phones were possible. Do you remember the first models, huge bricks of things with a long aerial? The world is changing rapidly. There is an international network actively promoting our device, people like your husband, Olivia, people of influence.'

'Really?'

'Oh yes,' Dennis said. 'We've even had diplomats arranging introductions in a host of countries and a number of serving soldiers are acting as salesmen at international trade fairs.'

Seemingly reassured, Mum forced a smile. 'Fair enough. Lead me to that food.'

Dennis's friend put on some music. There was laughter and conversation. Drink flowed freely. Before long, the buffet table had been picked clean. That's when the picture was taken, the one that ended up briefly on Mum's slideshow. Saffi was taking a nap and Mum was reading a magazine. My father and I leaned through the window, faces wreathed with smiles. Dennis's friend told us to pose for the photo and nodded when it was taken.

'I think we'd better get you home,' Dennis said.

A long, hot, lazy afternoon followed as we headed home through a clear, blue sea. Noticing the Sniffer locked away in its briefcase, I wandered over, opened the catches and walked up and down holding the handgrip. When the antenna swung suddenly, I frowned.

'I think we'll put it away now,' Dennis said. 'You've not been trained as a handler, Nick.' He changed the subject. 'There's ice cream.'

I was soon tucking into Ben and Jerry's Chocolate Fudge Brownie. The Sniffer was forgotten.

THE PROMISE

By the time I wake again, my father has joined Mum and Saffi.

'Saffi, love,' Mum says, 'would you mind getting your dad and me a coffee? Not from the machine. It's awful stuff. You know where the café is.'

Saffi gives them a cheerful smile, collects the ten-pound note Mum is offering, and sets off down the corridor. Mum leans into my father and brings him up to speed in a low whisper.

'I've been thinking about Harry Dennis.'

My father looks anxious.

'You didn't say anything, did you?'

'No, I managed to bite my tongue.'

They both glance my way, unaware that I have heard every word.

'It was the Select Committee today, Nick,' my father announces with a cheery flourish. 'I wiped the floor with one of the witnesses. It's a bad idea to go up against Tim Mallory if you haven't done your homework.' He looks happier than I have seen him in some time. 'It will be on the news. Look, this is going to blow over. When the press get nowhere with their questions, they'll lose interest.'

'I just hope you're right. Some of the parents at the school have been giving me funny looks.'

'Let them. The press pack has got nothing.'

Mum moves her seat closer to me.

'Do you remember when your dad won the by-election, Nick?'

I see a woman in a blue suit approaching the microphone. The candidates shuffle into place. The returning officer spoke in a voice that sounded as if her nose was blocked. She started to read out a series of names and figures. Suddenly there was a loud cheer followed by applause. An elderly lady waved a plastic Union Flag.

'Did Daddy win?' Saffi asked.

'He won,' Mum said. 'Daddy's the new Member of Parliament.'

My father spoke. I was so proud. We all were. Clearing his throat, he started to speak into the microphone.

'It is a very great honour to be asked to represent this constituency. Yesterday I visited all sixty-five polling stations and I saw for myself that this was an exceptionally well-conducted election. I would like to pay tribute to all the election staff, the police and the returning officer.'

There was a ripple of applause. I started to clap, felt stupid and stopped.

'I could not have won this seat without the efforts of so many volunteers. My party chairman, our councillors, my agent and the office team have been fantastic. Most of all, of course, my family, my lovely wife Olivia, my children Nick and Saffi and my parents, have been my rock. I simply would not be here without you.'

The party workers turned towards us, laughing, smiling and applauding.

'We ran a local and very positive campaign,' my father continued. 'We talked about what our party has done locally and nationally, and what we will do in the future. No matter who is in office I will always be a voice for our area, first and foremost.

'I believe an MP should represent all sections of the community. I will do my best to fulfil this duty. Many of you will know that I served in Her Majesty's Armed Forces.'

Applause followed.

'I learned in action that anyone who puts himself

in a position of leadership is only as good as those who march with him. I also learned that when people put you in a position of trust, you must never let them down. You must not wilt under fire. You must not put your own interests before those of the people you lead. That would be the most appalling betrayal. I promise never ever to let you down. Thank you for all your support. The hard work starts now.'

He left the stage and started to struggle through the press of bodies towards us. The press pack was already surrounding him. He gave Mum a wounded look, but she shot him an encouraging smile. Do what you have to do, it said. We'll be waiting. He sighed and began the round of interviews. After forty minutes, he finally joined us.

'I'm not sure I'm ever going to get used to all this,' he said. 'I must have answered the same question at least half a dozen times. Can't they vary it a bit?'

Councillor Harris was with him.

'That was an excellent speech,' he said.

Grandad was reading something. 'It was very good,' he agreed. 'I don't remember that bit about the promise in the version we agreed.'

Dad grinned. 'That's because I added it while I was speaking. It came to me on the spur of the moment.'

'It was very good,' Grandad said. 'It had the ring of sincerity.'

'Absolutely,' Councillor Harris said. 'It sounded like you meant it.'

The smile vanished from my father's face. 'I did mean it.'

Councillor Harris patted him on the back. 'It makes for a good speech, Tim, but don't go doing it too often. You can have too much sincerity, you know.'

'Meaning?'

'Ever heard the phrase, you can't please all the people all the time?'

My father looked uncomfortable, knowing he had stumbled, but not quite sure how. 'Of course I have.'

'This is a big constituency,' Councillor Harris explained. 'It's full of people with opposing interests. You can't tell them all you won't let them down. If you're going to satisfy some, you have to disappoint the others.'

Grandad nodded sagely. 'He's got a point, Tim.'

'Maybe,' my father said, 'but I didn't go into politics to say one thing and do another. I intend to be true to my principles.'

Councillor Harris whistled through his teeth. 'A principled man, eh? Well, good luck, Tim. You'll need it.'

We finally escaped from the count and piled into the car.

'Don't pay attention to Councillor Harris,' Mum

said as we pulled away. 'It's good that you made your promise. Don't let them make you cynical, Tim. Stay true to your convictions.'

Dad nodded. 'I intend to.'

'Are you going to be Prime Minister?' I asked.

'Not quite yet.'

'When?'

He glanced at me in his rearview mirror.

'Give me five years.'

'Five years?' Saffi said. 'That's ages!'

Mum gave my father an admiring smile then looked over her shoulder at us.

'I hope you're both very proud of your dad.'

'We are!' Saffi and I chorused.

'I'm very glad to hear it,' Dad said.

He hung a left on to the dual carriageway.

'I love you both very much. I will do everything in my power to make sure you stay proud of me.'

I remembered what he had said in his speech.

'You'd never let us down, would you, Dad?'

He parked in front of the house.

'I will never let you down,' he answered. 'That's another promise.'

QUESTIONS

'Are you awake, Nick?'

It's my father.

'Nicky, can you hear me?'

I blink. He smiles thinly, glances over his shoulder and moves his chair closer.

'You're on the road to recovery. I feel it.'

Yes, me too. Your point being?

'Pretty soon your memory will be returning too.'

More than you know. Suddenly, he isn't really talking to me. He's talking through his own demons.

'I wonder how much you will recall. That terrible night. God knows, I'm not perfect, but I have always tried to be a good father.'

You were. The best. Then you betrayed everything I thought you stood for.

'The older you get, the more complicated life becomes. You're going to remember things, Nicky. Whatever you think you saw, whatever you think you heard, try to remember me for the good I tried to do.'

Where's he going with this? Life was uncomplicated once or maybe I was too young to make sense of the complications. My parents were Olympians. Being older than Saffi, being just that bit closer to that adult world, I wanted to understand the rules of the heavenly realm. I wanted to steal their fire. I never dreamed my childhood gods would one day topple from the altar and smash to pieces on the floor.

'I just hope you will find a way to forgive me.'

I find myself in another time, another world. I am at the door of his study. I must have been in my early teens, maybe a bit younger. It's hard to remember. At that age, I just wanted to be part of their world. I approached his room, but something made me pause. Mum was inside with him, standing with her back to me, facing my father. He was out of sight, but I could hear his voice. I remember that image, Mum in a summer dress, a sparkling bracelet round her wrist, padding round the house in her bare feet. The sunlight from the French windows in my father's study seemed to melt around her, as if she was an ethereal spirit, a kind of angel.

'Who was that?' Mum was asking. She glanced at the phone in his hand. 'Who were you talking to?'

My father's voice bounced back, dull and indistinct. There was an edge of impatience, mixed with guilt. 'Nobody.'

'Tim, you can do better than that. Your voice was raised.'

His reply had been hard to hear, but it was impossible to miss the deep breath he had just taken. It was evident he resented Mum's questions.

'Fine. It was a journalist.'

'Journalist?' There was a crack of concern in Mum's voice. 'What journalist?'

'She was from *Inside Report*.'

Mum glanced over her shoulder, but she didn't see me.

'*Inside Report*?' she said. 'I've seen it a few times. It does investigative reporting. Why would they be interested in you? They look into corruption and fraud.' Her voice trailed off. 'Tim, what is this?'

Corruption. Fraud. Young as I was, the words made my skin tingle with anxiety. I had reached an age when I understood their seriousness. Mum continued her interrogation.

'Is there something you need to tell me?'

For several moments there was no answer.

'What's going on?'

I heard the scrape of my father's chair legs on the wooden floor.

'They're asking questions about Harry Dennis.'

Harry Dennis. His name is fixed in my mind. He's at the heart of everything. I want to focus on the memory, retain every detail, but my father hasn't finished talking to me. He drags me reluctantly back into the hospital ward, from the confusing past to the broken present.

'Nick, if it hasn't come back to you already, you are going to remember things about me. You will . . .'

He wipes his eyes and struggles to find the words. If I was able to talk, I could provide them. The only reason you had anything to do with a man like that is, you didn't think he was a man like that. Well, maybe you should have looked harder. You've got researchers, haven't you? Couldn't you run a check? My father rests his forehead in the palm of his hand.

'God, what a mess. I thought I was doing good. I thought I was saving lives.'

He lapses into silence and I return to that afternoon outside his study. I stood in the wash of the sunlight, listening. Mum was talking.

'You're scaring me, Tim. What's this about?'

I knew by the sound of their voices that it was serious. I was starting to gain some insight into my father's world. I had learned that wrongdoing wasn't as rare as I had been led to believe as a child. It wasn't just the preserve of 'bad people'. It wasn't just a matter of a few rotten apples. Sometimes there were whole barrels.

There were MPs who had gone to jail, but that was supposed to be ancient history, wasn't it? I had always thought my father was part of a new chapter. That's what he said in his victory speech the night he became an MP. He was a hero, a man who had fought for his country and been decorated for it. He was going to clean up politics. He was part of the cure, not the sickness. He'd promised never to let anyone down.

'It's this bloody Sniffer,' Dad answered. 'There are doubts about its effectiveness.'

'I had an idea Harry Dennis was trouble,' Mum said. 'Didn't I warn you to be careful about that man?'

Mum glanced over her shoulder a second time.

'Just a minute, Tim.'

I knew what was coming. I think she had sensed my presence. I slipped out into the garden and started dribbling my football round the lawn as if I'd been there all the time. Saffi was reading. She looked up, frowned and returned to her book. I could hear Mum opening the French doors to check on us.

'Nick,' Mum called, 'Saffi, are you two OK?'

When we answered promptly, she seemed

satisfied and rejoined my father. I left my football in the middle of the lawn and crept back inside.

'Where are you going?' Saffi asked.

'None of your business,' I answered.

She shrugged her shoulders and turned the page of her book. 'You're weird.'

I returned to the hall and listened, knowing I was concealed from view by the shape of the passage.

'I felt there was something fishy about that man. He gave me the creeps right from the start.'

My father sounded wounded, almost defeated.

'There's not much point going on at me now, Olivia. The damage is done.'

A note of anxiety entered Mum's voice.

'There's damage? What exactly?'

I glimpsed a blurry image of my father stepping out from behind his desk.

'I don't know. It's just a string of questions at the moment, lots of questions. How long have I known Harry? What are the terms of the consultancy? What do I know about the way the Sniffer is manufactured?'

'I wish you'd never had anything to do with that stupid gadget.'

My father's voice was crackling with anger. 'That *stupid gadget* was supposed to save men's lives. I've seen the lads in Headley Court hobbling round on prosthetic limbs, learning to walk again, because we couldn't detect the explosives that maimed them. I thought I could do something to stop that happening.'

I could just make out Mum perching on his desk.

'So what's this investigation about? You say there's something wrong with the Sniffer?'

My father was still being evasive.

'Tim, there's no point withholding anything now. I need to know what kind of trouble you're in. This isn't just about you. You've got a family. You owe me an explanation.'

The doorway formed a kind of tableau. My father was part of it now. He rested his hands on Mum's shoulders.

'That's just it. I'm not sure myself. I don't think this reporter has got much hard evidence so far, but she sounds determined to get some. She seems to think the Sniffer isn't all it's cracked up to be. She said she was going to America.'

Mum had been fiddling with her hair. She stopped. 'The States? Why?'

'Harry ships the Sniffer in from some place in Ohio. The reporter is flying out there next week.'

'These things are manufactured in Ohio?' she asked.

'Yes.'

'And you don't know any more than that?'

My father shook his head. 'Not a thing, and our friend from *Inside Report* wasn't about to provide me with information. She was keeping her cards close to her chest. I've tried phoning Harry to get some answers from him, but he isn't picking up his phone.'

Mum's voice was crackling with concern. 'I don't like the sound of that.'

My father pulled her close and she leaned her head against his chest.

'Neither do I, Olivia. I get the impression he's avoiding me. You know what they say: there's no smoke without fire.'

'This is serious.'

'It's got me worried,' my father said. 'I just hope I haven't made the biggest mistake of my life. Why did I have to be in such a hurry to promote the damned thing?'

He started to answer his own question. 'I was convinced Harry was the real deal. You should have seen his list of contacts. He knew embassy staff across the world. I thought I'd just found a way to reduce the number of deaths from IEDs. This was going to save British and allied lives.'

He raised his eyes to the ceiling. 'It wasn't all philanthropy on my side. I suppose I saw myself as a knight in shining armour. I was going to gallop to the rescue of our gallant lads.'

'You were also getting paid for the consultancy,' Mum reminded him.

'I was a fool,' my father said. 'Pride comes before a fall, eh?'

Mum pulled away. 'I warned you about Harry Dennis. I just knew something was wrong. How serious do you think this is?'

My father shook his head. 'That's just it. I don't have anything to go on. This journalist thinks there are questions about the Sniffer's effectiveness. I don't know any more than that and Harry isn't answering my calls.'

'How many times have you rung him?'

He handed Mum his phone. She looked at the screen and scrolled down his missed calls.

'Tim, he's blanking you. Not long ago, you were getting calls from him all the time. I think this reporter's on to something.'

There's another interruption and I am back in the present. The door goes and my father straightens up, expecting to see Mum. It's Nurse Choudhury.

'Oh, it's you, Mr Mallory,' she says. 'Where's Olivia?'

He mumbles an explanation.

'The pneumonia is starting to clear up,' Nurse Choudhury says. 'He's on the mend. It's not just the blinking. His facial muscles have relaxed. I can see expression in his face.'

For a while I listen to my father talking to Nurse Choudhury, asking her questions. Losing interest in the conversation, I reopen the door to the past. My parents were talking again and my father wasn't making any effort to disguise his concern about Harry Dennis.

'They've got enough material to conduct an investigation. The programme's going to air in a couple of weeks.'

'Oh, Tim!'

'They've door-stepped Harry a couple of times.'

Mum glanced at Saffi and me. To begin with, Saffi was oblivious. I pretended to be reading the blurb on the back of my new PlayStation game.

'Do you feature in this programme?'

My father shook his head. 'Not so far as I know. They haven't asked me for an interview or anything.' He took a bite out of a round of toast and jam and drained his cup of coffee. 'It's not all good news.'

Mum tilted her head, waiting for an explanation.

'The broadsheets have started sniffing around. You know what Cantona said: "When the seagulls follow the trawler . . ."'

'You've just got to tell them the truth, Tim. You didn't know Harry Dennis was doing anything wrong.'

'They don't know that. Since the expenses scandal, people think the worst of politicians.'

That's when I noticed Saffi staring.

'What did Mr Dennis do?' she asked.

Saffi was sharper than I thought. She'd picked up on the sense of apprehension in the room the same way I had.

'Mr Dennis didn't do anything, darling. Don't worry about it.'

Mum could hardly have been less convincing. She caught my father's eye, telling him they should have been more careful about discussing this in front of us.

'But you just said . . .'

My father put down his cup. 'They may as well know, Olivia. It looks like Mr Dennis's invention isn't everything he claimed.'

'He's been selling a fake!' I exclaimed. 'Isn't that some kind of crime?'

'I wouldn't go that far,' my father said.

'Can you get into trouble?'

My father looked at me then at Saffi. 'Listen, you two, there's nothing to worry about.'

It was no more convincing coming from him than it was from Mum.

CRYING

There's excitement on the ward.

'It always happens when you visit,' Mum says. She's doing her best to sound welcoming. 'You must be Nick's good luck charm.'

There is a new warmth between them. What was it Mum said the last time Maria came?

I may have been unfair to you.

You didn't have anything to do with Nick's accident.

I understand that now.

Maria gives a half smile. 'It's probably coincidence.'

She's squirming with discomfort at all the

attention Mum's lavishing on her.

'It's no coincidence,' Mum insists. 'It's you he turned to look at.'

So that's the big deal that had the medical staff crowding into the room. Maria was just out of sight and I turned my head to look at her. It's such a natural thing to do. It's a reflex action. You're interested in what somebody's doing. You turn and look at them. It's only a big deal when you've spent days playing at being Tutankhamun.

The doctor beams at Mum.

'This is very encouraging, Mrs Mallory. Nick's making such good progress. Your husband, will he be visiting soon?'

'Tim's at the Commons,' Mum explains. 'He's going to try to call in later.'

Mum's clearly itching to ask a question. 'So Nick's going to make a full recovery?'

'It's very promising indeed, Mrs Mallory. Would you like to discuss it?' She glances at Maria, then at me. 'Privately, I mean?'

Mum nods and follows her out into the corridor. Maria stares at the door for a few moments then rests her hands on her knees and takes a deep breath. There's something on her mind.

'It's wonderful that you're getting better,' she says. 'I just wish your mum wouldn't be so nice to me. It's my fault, Nicky. It's all my fault.'

OK, Maria, you've got my attention. What are

you saying? How can it be your fault? You're the best thing in my life. It can't be true.

'It was me,' she murmurs. 'I'm the one who made you crash.'

Whoa, whoa, stop there. Would you mind running that by me again?

'Oh, why did I have to run away like that? I was selfish, Nick. All I could think about was escaping the madness in that house. I didn't think about you and what you were going through. I didn't try to understand. I just ran.'

You ran. You left me with my father and that man.

'It was so dark, Nick,' she continued. 'Why did I have to panic like that?' She shakes her head. 'I couldn't see a thing. I just kept stumbling down the lane, losing my footing. I could have broken my ankle. Then I heard the car coming. I thought it was your dad. I wanted to get out of the way, but somehow I ended up stepping out in front of you.'

Suddenly, my mother's attitude to Maria was beginning to make sense.

'The headlights were dazzling. I just froze. I was paralysed with fear. I think I screamed and threw my hands up in an attempt at self-defence.' She laughs at the absurdity of it. 'Against an oncoming BMW! Who do I think I am, Wonder Woman?'

That's right. Yes, that's right. The image of a spectral figure bursts into my mind. Suddenly, there was somebody in the dark, a fleeing figure. I tore frantically at the wheel. So that's why I lost control. That's why she was so upset when she visited me for the first time. It wasn't just about my father. She thought she was to blame for the crash. There I am hurtling towards her in my father's Beemer and *she* feels guilty. Was I insane? Was I as crazy as the man with the dead eyes? I could have killed her.

But Maria isn't blaming me. She finishes her tale. 'It's all my fault. Nothing I did makes any sense to me now. Why didn't I stay with you? You needed me. The last thing I remember before you crashed was a glimpse of your face. It was such a look of horror. You twisted the wheel to avoid hitting me and careered into the tree. Nicky, I'm so sorry.'

Now I know who found me. Now I know who wrestled the door open and peered inside to see me slumped against the dashboard. It was Maria. It must have been several seconds before my father caught up.

My memory speeds back to just beyond the crash, before I saw Maria. I was at the wheel of the car. The woods were racing. Dead Eyes' voice was in my head.

When did you know?

The stark, black branches spread across the velvet sky like cracks. Everything blurred. Everything misted and fogged.

Get your murdering hands off me!

Maybe I imagined my father's hands on the steering wheel instead of mine.

Murdering hands.

But what made me run into the night in the first place? I didn't go with Maria. I know that. She didn't want me to follow. I suppose I had torn loyalties. I went back inside. What made me grab the keys and speed off down that potholed lane? It can't just have been the intruder's accusations. The man was unstable, crazy. Day after day, I've seen him standing at the bottom of my bed, screaming. How can I have taken anything he said seriously?

'Forgive me, Nicky,' Maria says, leaning forward to kiss me. 'I didn't mean . . .'

She dissolves into tears. I want to reach out and hold her. There's nothing to forgive, Maria, nothing at all. You ran. I ran. My father has been running for months, years. She dabs at her eyes with a tissue and glances at the door.

'Your mum will be back in a minute.'

She makes small talk for several moments then Mum returns. She's about to take a seat when her phone rings.

'Oh, hi, Tim,' she says. 'The text? Yes, I just wanted to tell you the wonderful news. Nick turned to look at Maria. Yes, he turned his head. The doctor thinks his recovery is well underway.'

Mum puts the phone to my ear and there's my

father's voice, excited, relieved, telling me he loves me. Mum puts the phone to her own ear.

'How long will you be?'

My father's voice crackles out of the phone's tiny speaker. I can't make out any of the words so I have to rely on Mum's side of the conversation.

'I tell you what,' she says. 'As soon as you arrive, I'll run Maria home and you and Nick can have some quality boys' time.'

■

My father arrives about an hour later. That's another sign that things are changing. I'm lucid for longer periods, allowing me to get a grasp of time. So this is part of my recovery. Boredom. I lie here, listening to Mum and Maria talking. It's trivia really, the kind of small talk that's only there to break the silence. My attention drifts and I start thinking about Dead Eyes.

I have a name for him now.

Not just Alec.

Alec Fraser.

In one way, knowing his name humanises him. He isn't Dead Eyes any more. He's no longer a monster, a looming mask of evil in the fog. Strangely, there is no comfort in these thoughts. He is not a monster. But he is a man who haunts me. Why is it my face I always see reflected in that pitiless stare? Something drives him. It isn't evil. It isn't savagery.

But it is just as destructive, just as implacable. It's here, locked in my memory, but I can't prise off the lid and look inside.

Do I really want to look into the box? Am I really that keen to face the reason I almost killed myself?

I know I don't have much choice in the matter. I'm mending. I'm going to find out whether I want to or not. There are times when I want to know everything and times when I want to curl up in a ball and block it all out. I hear my name and turn towards Mum's voice. She squeals with delight.

'Do you see, Tim? Do you see how much better he is?'

Mum kisses my cheek. This is new too. I can feel the press of her lips, the warmth of her breath. My gaze drifts to where my father is standing. It's hard to read his expression.

'It's such a relief, seeing him like this.' She laughs. It's an almost girlish sound. 'What am I doing? Just listen to me, Nicky. I'm talking about you as if you're not there.'

Don't worry, Mum. I'm used to it.

'I'll take Maria back now,' she says. 'You stay as long as you want, Tim. Talk to Nick. Tell him about your day.'

There is no response from my father.

'Let's go,' Mum says, sounding brighter than at any time since my accident.

Maria gives me a self-conscious kiss on the cheek

and follows Mum out into the corridor. Instantly, it's as if the temperature drops in the room. My father walks to the window and stands there, time hanging around him like a coat. Finally, he comes over.

'You're on the way back,' he says. 'Thank God. There were so many times I thought we had lost you. I know your mum has carried the burden so much more than me, but I don't love you any less. You must believe me.'

I feel like turning my head away to spite him. There is no physical reason I don't. Somehow, I lose the urge to punish him. I want to understand him.

'We're going to have to face what happened that night. We may as well start now. I suppose you've had time to think about it, Nick.'

He unbuttons his jacket and props his elbows on his knees.

'You see . . .'

He struggles to find the words.

'I know you were angry with me. I know you heard some things. It's just . . . It's like this. Alec Fraser suffered a terrible trauma, maybe the worst a man has to face in his life. He lost his only son. That kind of grief does things to your mind. You saw me hit him. Nick, it was self-defence. He was threatening me.'

That's not how it looked to me.

'He was threatening my family, you, your mother,

Saffi. I'm not proud of myself, but I had no choice. He was an intruder. He broke into the house.'

Broke in? No, he just walked through the door. You say you want us to face the truth, but you're twisting it.

'You saw him, son. He's mentally ill. I was facing a man who was unstable, potentially violent. What was I supposed to do?'

Unstable.

Potentially violent.

A portal opens and a different Alec Fraser walks into my mind. This is recent. A year? Six months? I'd walked from school to the library to get a lift home after my father's surgery. Alec Fraser was the last constituent to arrive, but he wasn't strictly a constituent at all. He didn't live locally. He'd travelled a long way. How do I know that? He must have mentioned it. There's the name of a town at the back of my mind. Birmingham? Leicester? No, it won't come. My father was guiding him out of the room where the surgery was held. My mum was edging towards the door.

'You can't fob me off this easily,' Fraser was saying.

I see a man in a worn off-the-peg suit, white shirt and tie. He is as neat and presentable as a man can be with limited money to spend. This isn't the danger man my father just described. There is pain in his eyes, but they're not dead. What happened to change that? My father looked uncomfortable.

'Mr Fraser, Alec, I'm not trying to fob you off.'

'You know Harry Dennis,' Fraser objected. 'You gave the Sniffer a recommendation. I've seen it on Securitaid's website.'

'That's right, Alec, I did. I accepted Mr Dennis's assurances about his product in good faith.'

'That's not good enough,' Fraser said. 'The Sniffer's completely useless. It's a piece of junk. *Inside Report* proved that conclusively.'

'There's certainly compelling evidence.'

I remember my father's evasiveness. I also remember Fraser's reaction.

'Compelling evidence! That's politician-speak. I prefer straight talking. Harry Dennis is banged to rights. *Inside Report* has handed the police a file of evidence.'

'Alec, the *Inside Report* programme didn't mention my name once. I don't know why you think I can help.'

'I just told you. You're on Securitaid's website. Don't try to tell me you're not involved.'

'There could be a court case, Alec. I really can't comment.'

There were a number of people milling about, watching the exchange. Some of them were starting to whisper. My father was squirming, just as he's squirming now. I hear a gargling sound. To my surprise, I realise that it's coming from my throat.

My father leans forward.

'What are you trying to say, Nick?'

He listens for a moment then sits up.

'Don't get yourself worked up, Nick. You're on the mend. You can't rush these things.'

Meaning what? You don't want me to rush back to health. Is that it?

'You're going to hear things about me, Nick. People are going to be throwing all kinds of wild accusations around. I acted in good faith.'

His chin seems to crumple. Is he going to cry?

'I was a soldier. I was a leader of men. My guys trusted me with their lives, Nick. Did I tell you about Ross McLeish? He took one in the leg in Helmand. I carried him back to the FOB under enemy fire. Does that sound like a man who would willingly expose a British soldier to danger? We were brothers, Nick, comrades. I would never, never betray a fellow soldier.'

He's struggling to control his emotions.

'The press is going to go after me. People I have worked with for years are going to turn their backs on me. All I've got left is my family. I love you, Nick. I need you to believe in me.'

That's just it. I don't. It tears me in half to say it, but I can't find it in me to trust you. Before my father can say another word, Fraser's voice wells up from the past.

'You're an MP,' he said. 'Somebody comes to

you with the magic bullet that's going to stop men dying because of IEDs. Didn't you think it was too good to be true? Didn't you think to look into it more carefully?'

My father sidestepped the question.

'I wasn't the only one who fell for Mr Dennis's scam.'

Scam? Some time earlier, my father was saying there were questions to answer. When did it become a scam? His neck was red. I could tell he was embarrassed by Alec Fraser's questioning.

'Maybe not,' Fraser said, eyes hardening, 'but that's hardly an excuse, is it? That's your face and your recommendation on Securitaid's website.'

'The moment I knew there was a problem with the Sniffer,' my father said, 'I severed all links with Mr Dennis and asked for my name to be removed from the website.'

'When?'

'I beg your pardon.'

'When did you tell him to remove it?'

I stared at my father. Tell him, I thought. You've got nothing to hide.

'I'm not sure exactly. I would have to check the dates.'

I was bewildered. My father has an amazing memory. That's what made him such a good MP. His mind was nimble. He regularly tied opponents in knots. So why didn't he just tell the truth? Fraser looked angry.

'Don't give me that,' he said. 'You know. Even if you're not sure of the exact date, you must have a rough idea.'

'Mr Fraser,' my father said, 'there could be legal proceedings. I will have to check the facts.' He said 'Mr Fraser'. It wasn't Alec any more. 'I have your number. I will be happy to discuss this with you further in due course.'

'Oh, you'll discuss it with me,' Fraser said. 'I'm not done with you yet, Mr Mallory, not by a long chalk. I want justice for my son.'

With that, he swept out into the evening.

'Dad,' I said, watching him go, 'who was that?'

'I'll tell you later.'

'Why not now?'

He was still looking uncomfortable. He leaned closer. 'Nick, people are listening. Can we talk about this when we get in the car?'

I gave my grudging agreement. Alec Fraser was climbing into a cab. I saw the look he gave my father as the taxi pulled away. It was anger, almost hatred. My father went over to Mum and they huddled in a corner. I could hear the sharp exchange of words.

'What's going on?' I asked. 'Who was that man?'

My father glanced at the onlookers then grabbed my sleeve, guiding me outside.

'Stop pushing!' I protested. 'What's going on? Who's Alec Fraser?'

'Nick,' my father said. 'Not here.'

We got in the car and drove off.

'Tim,' Mum said, 'not so fast. You're doing forty. You don't want another three points on your licence.'

He slowed down.

'He came all the way from Derby to grill me.'

Derby! That's it.

'He virtually accused me of killing his son.'

That struck me like a hammer.

'Killing his son! What are you talking about?'

Mum darted a look of fury at my father. She didn't like him blurting things out in front of me.

'We'll talk in the house.'

'You said you'd explain when we got in the car,' I protested. 'Now you want me to wait until we get home. Just tell me what this is all about.'

My father's jaw was set. 'We'll talk in the house.'

We drove the rest of the way in silence. All three of us were angry. My father swung the car into the drive, the chippings crunching under the tyres. The recriminations started the moment we got indoors. Mum was the first to speak.

'You should never have given that man the time of day, Tim. Harry Dennis is a chancer. Why didn't you listen to me?'

My father spun round to face her.

'I didn't want any more men to die. Don't you get it, Olivia? I thought I was doing the right thing. I thought the Sniffer was going to make a difference.'

Mum stood her ground.

'You thought you were going to impress senior figures in the party.'

'Olivia, do you really think I'm that cynical?'

Mum didn't answer. It was my turn to speak.

'Is anybody going to tell me what's happening?'

'When it comes right down to it,' he says, looking straight at me, 'all we've got is family. We've got to stick together, Nick. You, me, your mum, Saffi. It's us against the world. There are going to be people who want to throw me to the wolves. We have to stay solid. We have to be strong.'

And what if strength means lying for you?

■

I remember Mum ushering us into the kitchen.

'Let's sit down.'

I remained standing. I was still stinging from my father's rebuke.

'What's Securitaid?' I demanded.

My father's voice was flat when he answered.

'The company is called Securitaid International. It belongs to Harry Dennis's company. It markets the Sniffer RVX-80.'

'And you gave this thing your approval?'

'He misled me.'

'So you keep saying.'

My father's eyes narrowed, but he didn't rise to my sarcasm. 'Harry Dennis invited me to one of his demonstrations. It was very convincing. It could find drugs, tobacco, explosives.' He dropped his eyes. 'Maybe it was too good to be true.'

Mum snorted.

'But who was that man, Alec . . .'

His surname had slipped my mind. My father provided the information.

'Alec Fraser.'

'He mentioned some TV programme.'

'*Inside Report*,' my father explained. 'Seems it's been looking into Harry Dennis for months. They took the Sniffer apart in a laboratory. Apparently, it started life as a toy radio.'

'A toy? What's that got to do with bomb detectors?'

'Nothing.'

He saw the look of confusion on our faces.

'I know. It's just a lump of useless plastic.'

Mum's face was pinched with anxiety, but there was something else, a deep disappointment in my father.

'It gets worse,' he murmured. 'There are no moving parts in the tracker. The cards don't have any memory, any microprocessor. It's impossible for them to detect anything.'

'So the Sniffer's useless? It's just a piece of junk?'

My father closed his eyes for a moment.

'It's completely useless. *Inside Report* traced an expert. He examined the Sniffer and concluded it was pure random chance if the antenna pointed at anything.'

I recalled the way it indicated a point out at sea. *Pure random chance.*

'We've all been conned, Harry Dennis's customers, the people at the embassy, the soldiers he used to sell it at arms fairs . . . me. The Sniffer has been sold to governments all over the world. It's possible that security staff have died as a consequence.'

My flesh crawled.

'Died?'

'That's right,' Mum said. 'If a soldier or policeman has used the device to check for explosives and the Sniffer says the area is clear, an IED or car bomb can get through.'

Suddenly my mind filled with television images: rubble-strewn streets, soldiers, police and survivors picking through the debris, worst of all, the mangled torsos of the dead.

'Oh God.'

And here, in my hospital bed, the same words gargle indistinctly in my throat.

Oh God.

For several moments all I could do was stare. This was my father, the hero, and he looked completely washed up and humiliated. I understood that he had fallen for a scam and it could end his career. There was one thing I didn't grasp.

'Why did Alec Fraser come to the surgery?' I asked. 'What's he got to do with it?'

My father seemed to drag the answer out of the deepest depths of his being.

'Alec Fraser had a son,' he said, his voice hollow and sombre. 'He served with the Derbyshire Rifles in Baghdad.'

'Did you know him or something?'

It was as if there was a groaning sound behind me. A wall was about to fall.

'No, that's not it, Nick. Fraser's son was in a different regiment, posted in a different part of Basra. There was a checkpoint. The Iraqi security forces were using the Sniffer to check vehicles for explosives. They waved a car through. A bomber detonated a device hidden under the driver's seat. It killed an Iraqi policeman.'

'What about Mr Fraser's son?'

'Private Davey Fraser was on a routine patrol nearby. He was passing the checkpoint when the car exploded. He was in the wrong place at the wrong time.'

It was several moments before anyone spoke. The only sounds were the tick of the clock on the wall and the shudder of the fridge-freezer. Finally, I broke the silence.

'But why's Mr Fraser angry with *you*?'

'He thinks I should have said something earlier than I did. He thinks I should have gone to the press the moment I realised something was wrong.'

'But you didn't know . . . did you?'

There was a pause.

'That's right, son, I didn't know.'

And here, in my hospital bed, a word gargles in my throat.

'Liar.'

ON THE RACK

I sometimes feel like a torture victim, a prisoner drawn on a rack. Sensation has started to return. And how! I lie here with beads of perspiration standing out on my forehead. I want to scream, but I still don't have a voice, not really, just a kind of muddy gargle that people struggle to understand. There are two exceptions. One is Nurse Choudhury. She seems to grasp the odd word. As for Mum, well, she's Mum. She manages to get the general drift.

I'm not fixed in one rigid position any more. I can turn my head. I can blink. I close my eyes when I sleep, but that isn't often. It's the pain. There are moments when it's so intense it reminds me of a steel hook pulling out my insides. There are others when it's a low, gnawing pulse, throbbing, throbbing. With the trachy out, I'm able to force these low animal grunts out of my dry throat. I could talk, but I don't want to, not yet.

I've been lying here for hours, a sheen of cold sweat on my skin, bracing myself for each new pulse of pain. Gone is the thought that I'm going to curl up and refuse to surface. I'm on my way back. There's no reversing it now. I'm so tired of the hospital routines: the bloods, the IV, the physio, the pain relief that only takes the edge off it. I hate the bed bath the worst: the flannel rubbing my face, arms, chest, the hands rolling me over. I'm ready to be Nick Mallory again. I've constructed a kind of soft-focus video of the life I led before Alec Fraser walked to the bottom of my bed and cast his dead stare my way.

■

I heard a song on the radio once: you don't know what you've got till it's gone. Dead right. I took it all for granted, my spacious, comfortable home, my private school, my regular holidays provided by financially secure parents. Did I ever think about it? Did I ever consider myself lucky? It was natural. It was my entitlement. I had good friends in Theo and Victor. I played some rugby, did some cycling, devoted hours of my life to Call of Duty. I was going to say I chased some girls, but that all ended the day I met Maria. I'm ready to get my life back. I'm ready for everything about Mr Nick Mallory: the recovery, the barbed-wire noose of agony, the knowledge of what his father has done.

It's just the four of us today: me, Mum, my father and Saffi. 'Nick's looking so much better,' Mum says. 'Don't you think so, Tim?'

'He's definitely on the mend.'

I scrutinise my father's features. What do I make of him? He cares. I've seen the hurt and guilt in his face when he hears me moan with pain. If he was asked to have his body shattered and lie here in my place, he would. I have never doubted his love for me. But there is something else here. It is the way his gaze slides away when I try to catch his eye.

Is he afraid of me?

He doesn't look at me if he can avoid it. His gaze wanders around the room, skipping past my face. Am I any different? Both of us are torn in two. I don't hate him. I can't. Wouldn't it be easy if all I had to do was play the avenging angel and expose him before the world? But this is my father. All these years he has been my hero. Bring him down and look who gets crushed underneath the fallen colossus: Mum, Saffi . . . me. I destroy him and I destroy us all.

Saffi perches on my bed and starts telling me about something at school. She's bright-eyed, keen to help me 'snap out of it'. Gone is that look of fear she betrayed every time she looked at me. I'm surprised how much I look forward to her coming. I actually like my little sister. She's grown up in the course of this crisis. She shares things with me. I've even heard her making fun of Mum and Dad, mimicking their way of talking. She's got their gestures off to a T. Occasionally, and it is occasionally, she wonders out loud about that night and its fallout.

It's weird, discovering myself all over again. I'm walking through a stranger's life, finding it oddly familiar. This shell I inhabit, the Nick Mallory who went to school, attended some of his father's public engagements, had mates and a girlfriend, feels comfortable. He had a good life and that's what I want, the illusion in which I lived while my father destroyed its foundations. Suddenly, my attention shifts to the TV screen. It's the 6.30 p.m. regional news. Mum starts looking for the remote control. That's when I find my voice.

'No,' I croak, causing some widening of eyes. 'Leave it . . . on.'

This time, my words are clear. There is no ambiguity about their meaning. I suppose I've been building up to this for days.

'You're talking!'

'Ye-es . . .' I struggle to force out the next few words. 'Been able . . . for a while. I . . . want it . . . on.'

Man, does that hurt. I have to gouge out each word, ripping at my vocal cords each time, but it does the trick. Mum stares at my father. He nods, if without much enthusiasm. Saffi shifts her position slightly so that I can see the screen. The way she does it reminds me that she's as keen to know the truth as I am. It's the same two presenters who questioned my father the first time. Mum's not muting the news this time. I won't let her.

'I'm Abbie Thomas,' the female presenter says.

The man next to her on the red sofa smiles. 'And I'm Mark Dowling.'

The camera focuses on Abbie. 'Tonight we're returning to last week's news item, the MP and the businessman.'

'Yes, there's been a large postbag about this,' Abbie says.

My father slumps in his chair.

'The vultures are gathering,' he murmurs.

He doesn't even try to erect a defence. He lets us watch the report without comment.

'The question our report asked then,' Abbie continues, 'was this: how much did rising star Tim Mallory know about this man?'

There's Harry Dennis's face on the screen. This time it's a photo taken on the yacht, the same day my father and I were snapped with him. Harry Dennis is leaning back against the rails, looking plump and smug. Mark picks up the story. There's nothing new to start with. He goes through the details of the case: the fake bomb detector, my father's online recommendation of the device, the lives lost in Iraq and a number of other countries and finally the court case and Harry Dennis's seven-year sentence.

'Attention is now turning to this man, Timothy James Mallory MP, the Member representing Thames Valley West. When did he know that the Sniffer RVX-80 was fraudulent? This is what Mr Mallory told this programme seven days ago.'

They run the VT.

'Mr Mallory,' Abbie is saying in the clip, 'there have been allegations that you knew the Sniffer RVX-80 was quite useless much earlier than you have said.'

'That is not correct,' my father replies, leaning forward. 'The moment I knew that the device was ineffective, I severed all links with Mr Dennis and passed on what information I had to the relevant authorities, including the police.'

Abbie presses him.

'So not August eleventh? This is when the first allegations emerged about Mr Dennis. The date crops up in a recent television investigation. There was an alleged communication with your office from a regulator. Did you know then that the machine was in fact useless?'

'Definitely not.'

'Had you known then, you would have passed on the information?'

'I would,' my father answers. 'My only motivation in recommending the Sniffer RVX-80 was to save the lives of service personnel, both British and Iraqi. I am not the only one to be hoodwinked by Mr Dennis.'

'Indeed you're not, Mr Mallory,' Abbie says, 'but you're the only MP involved.'

My father picks at the crease on his trousers.

'That's right.'

'To avoid any doubt or ambiguity,' she says, 'can I put the date to you one more time?'

'I was able to confirm that the device was useless on March fifteenth,' my father says, interrupting her, 'a full seven months after the date you suggest. That's when *Inside Report* showed me conclusive evidence from the tests conducted in the United States. I immediately severed any connection with Mr Dennis and passed on what I knew to the authorities. I have nothing to hide.'

'I assume you are aware of the implications of what you have just told us,' Mark says.

'I am.'

'Your statement directly contradicts a story coming out of Baghdad.'

There is another VT. A middle-aged Iraqi stares moist-eyed into the camera and demands justice for his dead son.

'This man's son died because the security forces trusted a gadget you endorsed, Mr Mallory.'

There is a moment when the camera dwells on my father's face. Just for a second his gaze flicks away from Abbie. She spots it. He didn't know about the latest details emerging from Iraq.

'The family of a member of the Iraqi security services has alleged that you knew much earlier and that you failed to pass on the information. A well-known firm of human rights lawyers has taken up his case.'

'I've told you,' my father repeated, 'it's not true.'

Dowling persists. 'That charge has been repeated by this man, Alec Fraser, whose twenty-one-year-old son, Davey, died in a bomb attack on a roadblock. Both men's sons died during the autumn of that year.'

'I am entirely aware of the implications,' my father says. 'Before I go on, may I express my condolences publicly to the families of both men.'

Dowling nods. 'Of course.' He hesitates for a moment before continuing. 'Now, what do you have to say about this accusation?'

'I can confirm the date on which I knew for definite about the Sniffer. That was March fifteenth. I did not know any earlier than that. I was unaware of the accusations that had begun to surface. I have done nothing wrong.'

'And the email to your office?'

'I have no record of it.'

The clip ends and Abbie turns to camera.

'There you have it. Mr Mallory, MP for Thames Valley West, is insisting that he has done nothing wrong. Let's go over to our political correspondent in Westminster, Amrita Singh. Amrita, you heard what Tim Mallory said in that clip. What are the implications for his career?'

I watch my father's face carefully. He's giving nothing else away.

'It's very simple, Abbie,' Amrita says. 'If Tim Mallory knew on August eleventh and not March the following year that the Sniffer was unable to detect explosive material as has been alleged and failed to disclose the fact, it can be argued that he is at least partly responsible for the deaths of several members of the Iraqi security forces using the device and at least one British soldier.'

Next to me, Saffi starts crying. Mum comforts her.

'Don't, darling,' she says. She glances at my father. 'Tim, I'm taking her out. She shouldn't be listening to this. Come on, Saffi, let's get you something to drink.'

The door closes, leaving me alone with my father. Amrita Singh is still explaining the consequences.

'In that case,' she says, 'his position would be untenable. It is possible that he could even face a criminal investigation.'

My father picks up the remote control and mutes the TV. I can see his Adam's apple bobbing as he struggles to control his emotions.

'Nick . . .'

I interrupt him. 'It's over, isn't it? It's going to come out.'

'I don't know what's going to happen. Nick, I never wanted any of this to happen. What a lousy mess. I wanted to serve my country. I wanted to save lives.'

'But men died.'

'I know.' His voice fades to a whisper. 'Dear God, I know.'

Presently, Mum returns with Saffi. She's still red-eyed and subdued. Somehow, I can't let Mum and Saffi get hurt any more than they already are.

'Listen to me,' my father says, his voice cracking with emotion. 'We're in uncharted territory. I don't know how this is going to pan out. I didn't do this for personal gain, but I have opened myself up to some very serious charges. I just don't know what happens next.'

Saffi is still struggling with her emotions.

'Is there anything to it?' she asks through her tears. 'Why won't it go away?'

My father strokes her hair.

'I'm telling the truth,' he says.

The Saffi of just a few months ago would have

accepted every word. Now she sits stiffly, barely reacting to his touch.

'You're my family,' my father says. 'You're all I've got. I have to know you still believe in me.'

Mum rushes to reassure him. Saffi is a little slower to accept his offered embrace. When my father casts a glance my way, I turn my head and focus on the movement of the trees outside.

■

It was autumn. I remember the watery sunlight gradually clearing the mist, the sodden leaves underfoot, the slight chill on my cheeks. I was walking down the drive when I saw Mum and Saffi getting into the car. It was a crisp, cold day and there was the smell of cordite in the air from the previous night's fireworks.

The years have rolled back again. My memories used to surface chaotically, in torn rags. It's different now. I have summoned this one. We were still living in our old house. I must have just started secondary school.

'Did Jonathan's dad drop you off?' Mum asked.

'Yes.'

'Did you enjoy the fireworks?'

'It was brilliant, really professional. It was all synchronised to the music.'

Saffi rolled her eyes and pulled a *loser* face at me through the window. I shrugged and grinned. Mum braked at the main road then turned left. That's when I heard something smash. The noise came from inside the house. I frowned and opened the front door.

'Dad?'

He didn't seem to hear. There was no answer, no sound at all. I walked along the hall and paused at the study door. There was broken glass. I saw the mark where the tumbler had hit the wall and liquid had sprayed on the paintwork. I frowned at the scattered shards on the wooden floor.

'Dad?'

He was standing with his back towards me staring into the darkness. There were sweat stains on his shirt and there was something unusual about the way he was standing. Gone was the military bearing, replaced by a strange, diminished clumsiness. That's when I noticed the letter. The contents were only half visible where they had been roughly stuffed back into the envelope. The envelope had a Derby postmark, but it was the newspaper cutting inside it that got my attention. I remember the headline.

Soldier dead in Baghdad bomb attack.

I don't remember everything I read in that article. A few details linger: *Twenty-one-year-old Derby man . . . suicide attack . . . 1st Derbyshire Rifles.* I don't even know if I committed the dead man's name to memory. If I did, I soon forgot it. I know it now. It was Private Davey Fraser. I remember watching my father out in the garden, just staring into the distance.

'Dad?'

He didn't seem to register my presence.

'Dad? Are you crying?'

'Oh, my God, Nick,' he said through a voice thick with distress.

I stared up at him. By then, I was trembling, terrified by the trail of events that led from the stain on the wall, the broken glass and the letter to my weeping, tormented father.

'Dad, you're scaring me.'

I watched his fingernails travelling over his scalp. He seemed to be trying to inflict pain on himself. He seemed barely aware of my presence, in spite of having said my name.

'Is it about the soldier who died?' I asked. 'Was he one of your men?'

'This soldier, you mean? I didn't know him.'

This didn't make sense to me. Why was he crying over a stranger? He continued to scrutinise the letter. It was as if he expected some new revelation.

'You can handle a death in combat,' he said.

At that, I actually glanced round. Was I meant to answer? The words didn't seem addressed to me at all.

'But this . . . It's so senseless, so avoidable.'

'Dad, what's wrong?'

He couldn't say. He stared at me dumbly for the

longest time, then he put the letter away and forced out a few words.

'Ignore me, Nick. Are you hungry?'

I was still thinking about the letter and its impact on my father.

'A little maybe.'

'Look, son,' he said. 'Ignore me. Forget this ever happened. I'll get you something to eat.'

YOU TOOK MY SON

'**W**hat is it, Nick? What's wrong?'

Everybody seems pleased with my progress. I'm talking. I'm sitting up, beginning to sip fluids and eat some solid food. There's talk of me going home soon, though I won't be going under my own steam. I've got pins in one of my legs. The other has a clean break. Mum and Saffi are all smiles, though I can see the odd flicker of doubt in Mum's eyes. It could be about the speed of my recovery. It could be about the distrust between my father and me. Maria's the only one who isn't playing the game. She knows something's wrong.

'What's bothering you?'

I take her hand. Sometimes I marvel at how far I've come. Not long ago, a blink could take on epic dimensions, but the moment the switch was flicked, my recovery started to accelerate. Man, my body's starting to roar. I can hold Maria, and feel the warmth of her response. What was an impossible dream not so very long ago has become a small detail of everyday life.

I'm back.

You know what? It hurts like hell.

'I'll tell you soon,' I say, biting down on a surge of discomfort. 'There are things I have to work out.' I will her to understand.

'Take all the time you like,' Maria tells me. 'I'm not in any hurry to know what went on after I left the house that night. This is between you and your dad.' She hesitates. 'Isn't it?'

'Yes,' I say. 'That's about the size of it.'

There's the sound of footsteps. They stop outside the room. Maria and I watch the door then Mum appears. I try to second-guess the reason for her hesitation. Was she thinking about the future? Was she wondering how long my recovery would take or was she maybe piecing together the final details of the story of my father and Harry Dennis? Sometimes it's better to stay away from the truth.

'How are you feeling?' Mum says. 'Are you managing the pain any better?'

Managing the pain has got to be one of the

best euphemisms in the medical lexicon. It means bracing yourself while the vice of agony tightens, grips then loosens again. My pain is like the rhythm of the tides. It comes and goes, but when the waters recede you know they'll come again in just a few seconds. Sometimes the pain throbs. Sometimes it fizzes and buzzes. No matter what I do, no matter how I shift my weight or try to focus on something else, it's always there like a crow on a fence.

'I'm OK,' I tell her.

I haven't been OK for a while, of course. So when am I going to feel some kind of peace? It's so hard to know.

'You've got to say if it gets too much,' Mum says. 'It's all part of the healing process.'

Yes, keep telling yourself that. Every raw pulse of pain is a step in the right direction. Every time I wince, every time I grip the cotton sheet, it's another victory over oblivion. I'm here, I'm saying as I whine and suck in deep breaths. My mind is sharp. My body is healing. It's all worth it. Is it though? Is it really? Every day, I live with my memories.

I'm back in the house, the night I ran, the night I nearly died.

'You broke my nose!'

Somebody was roaring with outrage. Moments before, I had been sitting in my room with Maria, listening to music and talking. Then the voices startled us. It all happened so fast after that, Maria racing out into the night, me standing in the doorway wondering whether to follow then pursuing the sound of raised voices back into the living room. My father didn't see me to begin with. His attention was fixed on Alec Fraser as he bent forward over the sink, trying to staunch the bleeding.

'If I didn't know you were lying before,' Fraser said, his voice distorted by the bleeding, 'I do now. When did you know?'

When did you know?

All the time I was lying in my hospital bed, that question kept surfacing. My recollections of that night didn't come like a documentary, clear and sequenced. The whole thing was nightmarish, snatches of conversation echoing around me. It was as if I was in some macabre fairground ride and the confrontation downstairs kept clawing its way into my mind.

'How many times do I have to tell you?' my father said. 'I found out for the first time that the device was useless on March fifteenth.'

I remembered a November day and the smell of cordite. November. Four months before he was supposed to have known. He wept. He sat with a shattered look on his face and clung to a crumpled letter.

With such a look of guilt.

Dad?

'I ended my business relationship with Mr Dennis and . . .'

'Who do you think you're talking to?' Fraser yelled. 'Who the hell do you think you're talking to? I'm not one of your chums in Parliament.' He shook his head. 'Don't just go through the motions with me. I'm not playing games, Mallory. This isn't a committee hearing. I lost a son.'

'I know you did. It doesn't mean you can follow me to my home, Alec.'

Alec. It was Alec Fraser, the man with the dead eyes. I see the blood smeared on his face like lipstick.

'Don't tell me what to do! Don't you understand? That bomb ripped my boy to pieces. There was nothing in that coffin his mother could recognise.'

My boy.

The kaleidoscope of images revolves: the glass, my father's disbelieving gaze, the letter in his hand. The boy he wept over. It was Fraser's son.

'What do you want?' Fraser's voice was full of loathing. 'Are you really that stupid? I want justice.' He clenched his fists. 'That's all I've got left to hope for.'

My father had stopped talking.

'I've talked to the researcher at *Inside Report*,' Fraser said.

'She doesn't have any firm evidence,' my father said, just that bit too quickly.

I stared in disbelief. Why was he backing away like this? Why was he letting this man bully him? Fraser's face twisted with disgust.

'Firm evidence? This isn't about you wriggling out of an investigation. This isn't about the burden of proof.' He dabbed at his nose with his fingertips. 'This is about *my son*. You knew. I know you did.'

You knew.

You knew.

You knew.

Two words, repeated over and over, punching into my mind. But why was Fraser pursuing my father? Surely others were involved?

My father stepped forward. 'Mr Fraser, I have every sympathy for your loss. I served in the military.'

'I know that!' Fraser was wild with frustration. 'That's the point. I wouldn't expect any better from somebody like Harry Dennis. He's just a chancer who wanted to make a quick fortune. Do you think I have any trust in Whitehall bureaucrats and arms dealers? I trusted you.'

My father's face tightened. That got to him.

'The fact that you were one of us makes it worse. You're a decorated officer, Mallory. Some say you're a hero. You've pursued claims for lads who've come home mutilated by war. You've campaigned for better housing and conditions for servicemen. Do you know what the papers called you? The soldiers' ambassador. That's what bloody hurts. You were our champion and you betrayed us.'

'Mr Fraser. Alec . . .'

'No, you've had your chance. This isn't about you. This is about my boy, my dead son. It's about those mothers and fathers in Iraq who are trying to get somebody to listen.' He held up a photo. 'This is Davey. He was a soldier. I was a soldier before him. You let us down.' He stabbed a finger at my father. 'You should have known better.'

He took a step forward, struggling to get control of his emotions. 'I've lost everything.'

It was as if my father and Alec Fraser were one. There was a bottle and a glass. The glass shattered and their faces morphed into one.

I found myself willing my father to say none of it was true, to pull out some proof like a rabbit from a hat. He didn't. He was evasive.

'As I say, Mr Fraser,' my father said. 'I sympathise, but I don't bear any responsibility for it. Mr Dennis was a conman. I fell for his deception. I'm a victim too.'

The word *victim* exploded like a grenade.

'Victim!' Fraser looked incredulous. 'Victim, you? You got taken for a ride. My son *died*. And you could have stopped it.'

You knew.

You could have stopped it.

It was all coming back, the smell of the fireworks,

the marks on the wall, the broken glass, the discarded envelope.

'It was the day after Bonfire night,' I murmured.

Bonfire night.

November.

I remembered my father's anguish, his guilt.

'You said you didn't know until March.'

Neither man heard what I said. I followed the trail of my suspicions: the way my father pulled me close; his hacking sobs and anguished admission.

'He's right.'

Fraser was pounding his fists against his head.

'You knew!' he bawled, his face wet with blood and snot. 'You knew back in August. You had months to say something.' He snapped his fingers. 'You didn't say that much.'

His arms hung limp then he held up both hands and counted off the months, lowering one finger at a time.

'You knew in September, October, November.'

Yes, he knew in November.

Fraser sucked in a shuddering breath. 'That's when my boy died. That's when another family's son was torn to bits.' He continued the countdown. 'You knew in December, January, February. More lives were lost.' He stared at his hands. 'You kept quiet for seven months. *Seven months*! You didn't own up until March.'

My father tried to protest. 'Mr Fraser . . .'

Fraser screamed. His voice echoed through the house like the shriek of a trapped bird.

'Shut up. Shut the hell up!'

He tore a knife from the wooden block on the worktop and pointed it at my father.

The knife quivered in his hand. For a moment I could see it slashing, tearing open the fabric of my life. There was everything I loved like a canvas in an art gallery, being cut and cut and cut.

'Mr Fraser . . .'

'Liar! Murderer! People trusted that device. They waved bombers through checkpoints because they thought there was no danger to human life. Don't you have any decency, Mallory? Don't you have a single ounce of integrity?'

My eyes were blurring with tears. I relived the day my father hoisted me on his shoulders on a parade ground, the day everybody hailed him as a hero and the knife blade kept on slashing.

'How do you sleep?' Fraser demanded. 'You could have spoken in August. You had your chance in September or October.'

Or November.

His voice broke. His words were flaming brands. All those pictures I had of my father, in uniform, standing on an airfield with me on his shoulders, they started to blacken and burn.

'People would have listened to you. You could have saved lives. You could have saved my son.'

Still the knife shook in his hand. At the same time, I was stumbling forward mouthing the same two words.

'You knew.'

Still, they didn't see me or hear me. Fraser screamed, his mouth scarlet with drying blood.

'You took my son.'

At that moment, the tables turned. My father seized Fraser's arm and smashed it against the worktop, making him howl in agony. The knife flew from his grasp and clattered on the floor.

'Enough!'

That's when my father saw me and the blood drained from his face.

'Nick.'

Then there was the inevitable question.

'How long have you been standing there?'

'I've been there long enough,' I said. 'You knew.'

My father's lips parted, but I didn't want to hear another word.

'You knew!' I cried. 'There are people dead because of you.'

'No. Nick, no.' There was desperation in his voice. 'Even if I had said something, there's no guarantee they wouldn't have died anyway.'

'You could have tried,' I told him. 'You could have spoken out.'

'Nick, sit down and listen to me.'

I shook my head dumbly and stood my ground.

'Hear that?' Fraser said. 'Even your own son knows you're a liar.'

He broke free and stepped into the night. 'You haven't heard the last of me.'

Just for an instant a shaft of sunlight caught his face.

'You took my son, Mallory. I'll take yours.'

That's when it all got too much.

I ran.

HOME

I'm home.

In fact, it's been a few weeks. Now that I'm back at Forest Grange, I've had to get used to dark, quiet nights alone and the shapes of the trees outside.

There's one welcome change. I can have my window open and feel the breeze whispering through the curtains. The hospital was an artificial world with closed windows and a kind of headachey claustrophobia. I love the movement of the air in the curtains, the sense of all that quiet darkness just beyond the windows. I am able to pretend none of this ever happened.

The day I came home my father opened the door,

put my things on the hall table to sort later and stepped aside to let me pass. My progress was slow and clumsy. Once everyone was in, he scooped up the mail and we heard a groan of dismay.

'What is it?' Saffi asked, her face pinched and anxious as she hurried over to him.

'I've had another one.'

He handed the unopened letter to Mum.

'What's this about?' I asked.

'It's that man,' Mum explained, 'the one who lost his son.'

'Alec Fraser.'

She nodded.

'What about him?'

'He's been sending your father poison-pen letters.'

I leaned on my crutches and held out my right hand. 'Can I see?'

Mum held back.

'They're too upsetting,' she said. 'Alec Fraser must be going through hell, but the way he came to the house.'

The way he came to the house.

That was probably the first time I realised my father had finally owned up to Mum about Fraser coming to the house. Somehow, he's explained how they argued and I fled into the night. When did this happen? No, I decide, it doesn't really matter. He's told Mum enough to stop her asking questions, but not enough to know what he really did. I can just imagine the conversation. How many times did she ask him if he was hiding anything else? How many times did he swear on our lives that there was nothing more to confess? I remembered Fraser's dead eyes, the slash of his screaming mouth.

'His son died unnecessarily,' I said. 'Imagine living with that every day of your life. Something like that could drive you crazy.'

Mum ripped open the envelope and started to read. There was anger in the way she tore it, anger in the way she read. She bit her lip and marched down the hall, ripping it up as she went.

'There's only one place for this filth,' she said, her voice sharp, but tearful.

The pieces fluttered into the wastepaper basket in the living room. I glanced at my father and followed in Mum's footsteps.

'How long has this been going on?'

'Weeks.' She was fiddling with a tissue. 'The letters were coherent to begin with, angry but they kind of made sense. They've just got worse and worse. They worry me.'

My father walked into the room. An unspoken communication passed between them. I didn't say a word, not in front of Mum and Saffi. There was no point upsetting them. My father was the one who would have to tell the truth, not me.

'I know he's suffered a tragic loss,' Mum said, 'but it's becoming an obsession. Harry Dennis is the one to blame.'

There was an uncomfortable silence then my phone rang. It was Maria calling during her lunch hour at school.

I was still feeling edgy about my father and Fraser's letter. Did I let it show? Maria didn't seem to notice.

'I'll be round after school,' she said. 'We can spend some time together.'

I smiled and put warmth in my voice. 'Sounds good.'

So that was it. I was home. Mum was right. It hasn't taken me long to get used to the crutches. To begin with I went upstairs on my backside, using my arms to negotiate them. As my muscles have repaired, I've been able to go up and down on my crutches. Mum's always telling me to be careful, but I'm getting confident, cocky even. I go for walks round the grounds with Maria. We visit the oak tree sometimes and stare at the scarring.

'You could have been killed,' she says.

'I wasn't though, was I?' I touch the marks where the car tore the bark. 'You know the way people used to carve their initials in trees?'

'I don't think you should do that,' Maria says. 'Trees are beautiful.'

'I wasn't going to,' I tell her. 'This is a reminder

that I was here. Maybe it will still be here long after we're all gone.'

She puts her arms round me.

'Don't get morbid on me,' she said. 'It's a reminder you survived.'

'I feel as if I left something behind when I had the crash.'

'You're making an amazing recovery,' she says. 'I was the one who found you.'

I squeezed her waist.

'I know.'

'I'll never forget that sight.'

'Don't dwell on it,' I tell her. 'That was then. This is now. It's over.'

I hear my own words and wonder whether it will ever be over. Will Dead Eyes ever stop screaming? That's right, he still comes to my bed from time to time. I know it's not the real man of course. It never was. Fraser's told his tale. The police have looked into his claims that my father colluded with Harry Dennis, that he is equally guilty. There's insufficient evidence to go any further, they say.

There are only four people who know the truth. One is Harry Dennis. He's appealing against his sentence so he's keeping quiet. There's my father and Alec Fraser. Then there's me. I'm not saying a word either.

I'm back in school, have been for some time. It's good to have a pattern to my days. For so long, in hospital, they were shapeless, a canvas of pain and jumbled memories. I swing along the corridors at quite a lick these days. The PE teachers have been asking about my legs. Will I be able to play rugby again? I don't know what to tell them. The pins are staying in my right leg. Will I ever run as fast as I could before the crash? Beats me.

Like they say, I'm taking a day at a time.

The questions about my father's conduct have slipped out of the news. *Inside Report* seems to have given up its pursuit for now. It's the police decision that there's insufficient evidence, I suppose. They've got nowhere to go with the investigation. It's an uneasy truce, the rival troops shouting to each other across no man's land. Only we don't shout. We don't really talk all that much, certainly not my father and me. Saffi thinks things are back to normal. I know differently.

Saffi watches TV while Maria and I do our homework together. We're in the kitchen, with our books spread out on the table.

'Things are still tense between you and your dad, aren't they?' Maria says.

I look through the arch into the living room, where Saffi is curled up on the sofa, head on the arm, staring at the screen. She can't hear us and there's no sign that she's even interested in what we've got to say.

'Everybody's got secrets,' I observe.

Maria places her hand on mine.

'I'm not fishing. It's OK if you don't want to share.'

'I'll pass on that, if you don't mind. Do you want something to eat?'

I shift my weight and reach for my crutches.

'That's all right,' Maria says. 'I'll do the honours. Sandwich?'

Almost without thinking, I return to the night of the crash.

'My father's behaviour really freaked you out, didn't it?'

'It was the way he hit that man. It was a side to him I'd never seen before.'

I grunt dismissively. 'That goes for both of us.'

'Nick,' Maria says, 'I'm so sorry I ran. Maybe if I'd stayed, things would have turned out differently.'

'Some people stand and fight,' I said. 'Most people run.'

'Cowards run,' Maria said. 'I should have stayed. If anything ever happens again, I won't run.'

'Nothing's going to happen,' I tell her. 'We've had more than our share of craziness.'

Maria's mum picks her up about ten. I'm in the bathroom later, brushing my teeth when my father's voice echoes up the stairs.

'Olivia, can you believe this?'

'I know, Tim. I know.'

'I thought it was finally blowing over then Fraser shows up at the meeting.'

I rinse my mouth and frown into the mirror.

'He must know I didn't mean for any of this to happen,' my father says. 'I would never put anyone in danger. Surely, he understands.'

'Should we be worried?' Mum asks. 'I'm thinking about the kids.'

'We've got to take our security seriously, Olivia. Did you see the state of him? He didn't look like he'd washed for a week. I couldn't believe the condition of his clothes.'

My father pours a drink. I can hear the whisky clink in the glass.

'What does he want? What more am I supposed to do?'

My hands tighten on the sink as I listen. I know what he's got to do. He's got to give Fraser justice. He's got to tell the truth.

'I've had the local news on my back, Olivia. I've had *Inside Report*. I've even had the police and Party Head Office. It's gone on and on. I made a mistake, but it's turning into a witch-hunt. Am I meant to lie down and die? I've answered every question they've put to me. I just want to get on with my life.'

I rinse my face and cross the landing to my room. I'm about to close the door when the phone rings. My father takes the call in the kitchen. I can hear his side of the conversation.

'Hi, Dad. I know, it was unfortunate.'

. . . 'What were people saying after I left?'

. . . 'Peter Harris did? Good on him. So Fraser's outburst hasn't done any lasting damage?'

. . . 'No, Dad, I'm not concealing anything. Fraser wants something none of us can give him. He wants his son back.'

What Fraser wants is justice.

■

A few weeks later I have my final visit to the hospital. The doctor consults his computer and looks at my X-ray. He seems happy with my progress.

'Getting any pain?' he asks.

I shrug. 'Not much. Sometimes I take a paracetamol before bed. That's about it. I just don't go kicking cats.'

The doctor smiles.

I ask about rugby. He seems to think I'll be able to play in time, but maybe not at the same level.

'You're disappointed,' he says.

'It's nobody's fault, but mine,' I answer.

Mum drives me home. We both see Fraser at the same moment.

'Oh no.'

He's standing on the corner of the drive, brandishing a homemade placard.

'Could you read what it said?' Mum asks as she swings past him into the drive.

I say the words slowly.

'Mallory. Liar.'

I wait a beat before reading the final word.

'Murderer.'

Mum parks the car in front of the house and we walk across the tarmac to the front door. We both pause on the step to glance back down the drive.

Once inside, she picks up the phone.

'What are you doing?' I ask.

'I'm going to call the police to move him on.'

I take the phone from her.

'Don't, Mum. Please. He's lost his son.'

She lets me take the phone and put it back in the cradle.

'Why can't he just leave us alone?' she asks.

'I don't think he can. His conscience won't let him.'

I see the way she stares at me.

'There was a fight.'

Mum leads the way into the living room and peers out of the window, looking for some sign of Fraser. The woods are empty.

'I know. Your dad's told me everything.'

Everything? I don't think so, Mum. He's told you about Fraser coming to the house. He's told you about the accusations. He couldn't wriggle out of it. He hasn't told you that he knew about the Sniffer and that he let those men die.

'Nick, have you got something to tell me?'

She's scrutinising my face, trying to read my thoughts.

'No, Mum, there's nothing more to tell.'

'If there's anything, Nick, anything at all, you have to talk to me.' She looks me in the eye. 'I'm going to ask you one last time: is there anything you want to tell me?'

I squeeze her arm and turn to go.

'No, Mum,' I say, 'there's nothing.'

HERE COMES THE NIGHT

'**Y**ou're only jealous.'

I watch while Saffi packs.

'I'm not arguing with you,' I confess, perching on the bed. 'School trip to France. I'm dead jealous.'

That seems to make her happy. She's grinning like a Cheshire cat.

'How long are you going for?'

'Only five days,' she says, folding a pair of jeans and laying them carefully on top of the rest of her clothes. There's a moment of urgent realisation as she remembers something. 'Oh, hair straighteners.'

'Don't panic!' I cry. 'No need to panic. Call off the F-16s. She's got the hair straighteners.'

She swats me with them.

'Hey, watch it,' I protest. 'Didn't you know there were 27,000 hair straightener-related accidents in British homes last year, fourteen of them fatal?'

'Nick, you're so lame.' She taps my crutches with her toe. 'When are you getting rid of these things?'

'Not long now,' I say. 'A couple of weeks maybe.'

'So you're nearly healed?'

'Nearly.' I hoist myself to my feet. I've pestered her long enough. 'When do you go?'

She pulls a face. 'We're leaving here at five in the morning. The coach leaves school at six. No lie-in for me.'

It's my turn to pull a face. 'Ouch. Well, keep the noise down. I don't need to get up until seven.'

Saffi zips her case. 'Rub it in, why don't you?'

I'm about to go when she tugs at my sleeve.

'Something bothering you?' I ask.

'I don't know,' she says. 'It's you and Dad.'

'What about us?'

'You used to be so close. Now . . . you don't talk.'

'We talk.'

Saffi shakes her head.

'No, Dad talks. You grunt. What is it between you two? Is it still about the time Fraser came to the house, all this stuff with the Sniffer?'

I shrug. It's something I've become good at.

'Maybe he's not who I thought he was.'

Saffi's not happy with that.

'He's still our dad, Nick.'

I don't want to have this conversation. She doesn't know the truth. She mustn't know the truth. In the best of worlds, I would force my father to come clean. I want to tell her everything, but it would break her heart. It could tear my parents apart. Mum's said it herself. She couldn't take any more lies.

'Don't be too hard on Fraser. He lost his son.'

'That was Harry Dennis's fault ... and the bomber's. Dad didn't have anything to do with it. The police cleared him.'

These are the moments I have to bite my tongue. I want to say what he did. I want to clear my conscience. Instead, I nod.

'Yes, the police cleared him.' I force a smile. 'Have a good time in France, Saffi.'

She smiles back, her face still troubled. I know that look, that sad, uncertain place when truth trembles, before retreating behind the disguise.

'Thanks, I will.'

∎

She's gone by the time I get up. Mum's back after dropping her off. She's busy making me a bacon sandwich for breakfast. I could do it myself, but she likes waiting on me hand and foot. It's a legacy of the accident.

'Are you doing anything today?' I ask.

'Providing a taxi service for my children,' she replies, cutting my sandwich diagonally and putting the plate in front of me.

'After that?'

'I'm working at home,' she says. 'I've got a spread to finish.'

'Are you in it?'

She pulls a face. 'Do I look twenty years old? No, it's about some of today's emerging stars. Advice from a veteran of the scene.'

'You're a veteran?'

'I have to dye out the odd grey hair so yes, I'm a veteran. You'll have to make yourself something this evening. We've got the dinner at Redlands.'

I take a bite of my sandwich. 'Dinner?'

'Peter Harris is standing down as leader of the council. His wife had a stroke. He's retiring to take care of her.'

The story's familiar.

'Oh yes, I forgot.'

'You'll be OK here, won't you?'

'Yes, of course.'

'We won't be late,' she says.

∎

The late afternoon drizzle has developed into a heavy downpour by this evening. Through the rain-dimpled windows, I can see the trees tossing in the wind, the gloom of the woods. I am walking without the aid of my crutches. The doctor says it's just a matter of gradual healing. That made me smile at the time. The doctor didn't understand.

For some reason, I'm restless. I try watching TV, but I just surf aimlessly before switching the set off again. I pick up a book. I glance in the fridge for something to eat, but I don't make a sandwich. My mind is elsewhere, out in the roaring blackness of the woods.

I pace the floor unsteadily, wondering whether I might need my sticks after all, when fear chills my flesh. I just saw movement out of the corner of my eye. I twist round and there he is, walking through the kitchen door. Fraser has steam rising from his shoulders, his expression somewhere between vacancy and despair. He must have been standing in the rain for some time. I make a grab for my phone while I've still got time. Praying he won't see me, I start to call my father.

He's a scarecrow. His hair, though damp, is straw-brittle. His skin is parched and rough with stubble. His lips, pale and bloodless now, are cracked. Then there's the detail with which I'm all too familiar, the dead eyes, ringed with darkness. I need to distract him, while I finish the text. I force myself to ask the obvious question.

'What are you doing here?'

He doesn't speak, but I already know the answer. *You took my son, Mallory. I'll take yours.*

'Mr Fraser,' I begin.

He barks a command. There are no neighbours to hear.

'Shut it! Shut your lousy, filthy mouth.'

I finish the text and send.

'What?'

His hand slips behind him. I know instantly what it means.

'Please don't do anything stupid.'

That's when I see what he's holding, a survival knife with a black handle and a serrated edge. His arm hangs and the knife hangs with it. He glimpses the phone.

'Hand it over. I don't want any interruptions.'

The knife hasn't moved. This is a man who is agitated and unstable, but his hand is steady. It's a combination that's got me very anxious. I swallow. He moves the knifepoint a few centimetres closer to my face.

'Let's have it.'

His eyes are without empathy. His hand is still steady.

'Get me your house phone too.'

I'm reaching for it when it rings. Fraser uses the knife to wave me away from it. He sees the caller ID and smiles.

'Well, if it isn't Mr Mallory. It saves me having to ring him.' He answers the phone. 'That's right, Tim, it's Alec Fraser. You got a text?' He looks my way.

'Clever boy, Nick.' He turns his attention to my father. 'What am I doing here? What do you think? There's no need to rush, Tim. Nick and I are getting along just fine. I won't do anything until you get here.'

My father's voice is barely audible, but I can guess what he's saying.

'Are you threatening me, Tim? That's not a very wise thing to do now, is it? Where are you anyway? Is that right? How long will it take you to get home, twenty minutes, half an hour? Drive safely now.'

Fraser cancels the call, opens the fridge and swigs from a carton of orange juice.

'He's worried about you.'

I scowl, trying to sound brave. 'I can take care of myself.'

A shadow passes across Fraser's face.

'That's a strange thing to say under the circumstances. I thought you'd be yelling for him to ride to the rescue.'

Then, very slowly, he starts to smile. 'You know, don't you?' He's moving the knife, slowly tracing a number eight in the air.

'Daddy the fraud. Daddy the liar. Daddy the killer. Now here's the son following in his footsteps.' He drains the carton and drops it in the bin. 'Would you like me to tell you a story, Nick?'

'I know what you're going to say.'

'Is that right? Well, I'm going to tell you anyway.

Once upon a time there was a soldier. He wanted to fight for his country. His enemies wanted to kill him, but he expected that. What he didn't expect was for another soldier, an officer no less, an MP to boot, to join forces with some lousy fraudster and sell fake bomb detectors.'

'Alec . . .'

'Shut it!'

The knife continues to weave its lazy pattern, reminding me that he's holding all the cards.

'Well, the fraudster gets caught, but the officer, the MP, he's too clever to get caught. He knows the bomb detector's useless, but he doesn't do anything. He doesn't do anything for seven long months . . .'

'Alec . . .'

'Shut . . . your . . . lousy . . . mouth!'

The knife is almost touching my throat.

'Just shut the hell up.'

Fraser has got the knife in his right hand. With his left he is rubbing the phone compulsively against his temple. His eyes focus on the phone.

'You rang him.' He's talking slowly, dream-talk. 'Daddy's coming. At this very minute he's racing to save his boy.'

His dead eyes are on mine.

'He took my son. He took Davey.'

'No,' I say. 'It's not true, Alec. Whatever my father said or didn't say, he didn't kill your son. The bomber did that. It's Harry Dennis's fault that the bomber got through.'

'And Mallory's! Your dad could have saved Davey.'

I drop my gaze.

Fraser's got the knife moving up my face, pressing against the rim of my eye socket.

'Well, here's how the story ends, Nick. It's in the Bible. An eye for an eye. Mallory took my son. I'm going to take his.'

'Alec,' I say, the full horror of what he has just said numbing me. 'You don't need to do this.'

'But that's just it. I do. Don't you see? This is such an exciting story. Daddy's rushing to save his boy. He's driving far too fast. I hope he doesn't set off that speed camera on the hill. He should be here any moment.' There's the hollow laugh again. 'Maybe Daddy will glance at the tree where his boy almost died. He'll scream to a halt out there. He will run and run, heart banging. He'll reach the door.'

Fraser dangles a key in the air.

'Just one problem, the avenger locked the door. That will give me just enough time.' The knifepoint is pressing into the skin under my eyeball. 'An eye for an eye.'

Fraser makes a grab for me. I try to struggle, but he kicks me hard. Instantly, a wave of pain washes up my leg. He's strong. His arm is round my neck and the knife is back against my eye socket. A second time, I start to struggle.

'Not yet, Nick. It's too soon for the finale. We wait until we see the lights of Daddy's car, then we can have the big finish. An eye for an eye. I want him to see.'

'Alec,' I say, finding it hard to get the words out because of the threat of the knife, 'listen to me. Don't do this. I haven't done anything. Two wrongs . . .'

Fraser interrupts. 'Two wrongs don't make a right, is that what you were going to say?' He chuckles coldly. 'Why not? Why the hell not? You're a chip off the old block. Daddy kept shtum. You did too. Bad seed, you see.'

He tires of me trying to squirm free and kicks me again, viciously and with such force I howl with pain. It's like magma belching up the throat of a volcano, molten, hot, unstoppable. This time Fraser has miscalculated. Such is the pain I break out in a cold sweat and fall against him, throwing him off balance. We crash to the floor together. Just for a moment, the knife spins out of his grasp. I'm on my back, lying on top of him. If only I can turn. If only . . .

He's got the knife back. He's got his fingers in my hair and he's pulling me back. At the same time, he's trying to twist the blade round and hold it against my throat.

'Stop fighting me. I'm a soldier. I'll make it quick.

But not yet. We've got to wait for Daddy. I want him to see. I want . . .'

I manage to free my right arm and smash my elbow into his face. I hear the moist gasp as it crunches into his mouth. I roll clear and see the scream. His mouth is nothing but a slash. And I freeze. It's this image. It's been with me all this time. My moment's hesitation means I squander my advantage. Fraser's got his arm round my neck again. He's spitting blood over both of us and fighting to get the knife against my throat.

'Nice try,' he splutters. 'Good, but not good enough. That was stupid, Nick. I was hanging on for dear old Dad, but you've forced my hand.'

The knife is at my throat.

'Let's get this over with.'

There's a crash. What the hell is happening? Broken glass sprays both of us, glittering around us as we lie on the floor. Simultaneously, there's yelling in my ears. It's Fraser's moist, visceral howl of rage. Then there's the most amazing moment of freedom. There's no pain. There's no knife at my throat.

I turn to one side and there's Fraser, his eyes closed, the dead look gone. My father is kneeling over him.

'Is he . . . ?'

'He's unconscious. I did what I had to.'

'There was no light.'

'I didn't want to warn him,' my father explains. 'I knew he was unstable. I had to take him by surprise so I parked halfway up the lane and ran the rest of the way. The door was locked. I had to smash the window to get in.'

Then there are headlights and confusion. People are crowding into the room. Mum's there. The police. Paramedics.

'I hurt,' I say. 'I hurt really bad.'

Mum kisses me through the blood. She kisses the blood.

'Just rest.'

And that's what I do.

I close my eyes.

But not for ever.

THE END

The police finally leave about half past nine. Their vehicles go one by one, their tyres hissing on the rain-slicked drive. Fraser wasn't badly hurt, at least not on the outside. I've been broken, in mind and in spirit. I think I've got some sense of the Furies that pursue him. For a few moments I listen to the rain falling in the woods. My life changed for ever because of something that happened out there in that dripping darkness. I was lost. Maybe tonight I've found myself again. Finally, I turn and make my way back into the living room where my family is gathered. I stumble for a moment and Mum rushes to steady me.

'Are you all right?'

'I'm fine,' I say, doing my best to reassure her. 'My legs are a bit bruised, but I've been worse.'

The house is silent at last, empty except for Mum, Dad and me. So I get my chance.

'You've got to resign, Dad.'

I hesitate for a moment. When did I start calling him Dad again?

'Is there something wrong?' Mum asks, anxious as ever.

'I'm fine. I've got something to say, that's all.'

I think Dad knows what's coming. He gives me a reassuring nod.

'Carry on, Nick.'

'You've got to resign.'

There's no response, not from Mum, not from Dad.

'You said it yourself, Dad. You said you would never let us down. You refused Alec Fraser justice. I'm not saying this to hurt you. Dad, if I hurt you, I hurt myself. I looked up to you. No, it was more than that. I worshipped you. You were everything I wanted to be.'

My father's face is a mask of misery and self-loathing.

'You've got to make it right, Dad.'

'Tim,' Mum says, 'maybe you should sleep on it. There's no reason to rush into things.'

Dad shakes his head. 'Nick's right. I've nothing

but contempt for the man I see in the mirror. I can't sleep. I haven't slept properly since the accident. I haven't been able to look my own son in the face. When I was elected, I swore to be a different kind of politician. I was never going to let people down. Well, you're right, Nick. I've done just that. There's only one way to clear up the mess. I've got to go.'

'So what are you going to do?'

'Something I should have done months ago.'

He searches for his laptop case, turns the machine on and starts typing. The letter will go to the Prime Minister the following morning.

■

It's a bright day when my mum and dad, flanked by Saffi to the left, me to the right, stand on the front steps of our house in the woods, while the media pack presses forward.

'I have a statement,' my dad says. 'You will have read my letter to the Prime Minister, offering my resignation as a Member of Parliament. There isn't much to add, just this. I was a soldier. I led my men under fire. I got involved with Mr Dennis because I thought I could help to save the lives of men like the ones under my command. I made a catastrophic error of judgement and compounded that mistake by failing to reveal what I knew about the RVX-80 until several men had lost their lives. I let down the Iraqi security officers. I let down Davey Fraser. I let down his father, Alec Fraser.' He looks up from his notes and speaks without them. 'Davey Fraser put on a uniform to serve his country. He knew he would face his enemy. He was ready to take the consequences of his choice. What he did not deserve was to be let down by people who would decide his fate because of flawed decisions, people like me. When Alec's case comes to court, I will be making a statement in his defence.'

A murmur runs through the crowd of reporters.

'Finally, I let down the people who voted for me and I let down my family. My son Nick has shown a commitment to the truth I signally failed to. After the events of the night before last, he told me what I had to do. Today, I am finally telling you the truth. Politics should be about the will of the people.'

The reporters start shouting questions. My father shakes his head.

'I'm not answering questions. I would ask you all to respect our privacy.'

He leads us back indoors. Saffi rushes upstairs, visibly upset. Mum follows her.

That leaves my dad and me alone in the hall.

The last members of the press pack are leaving. Two of the reporters watch us as they climb into their cars. We stop to let them manoeuvre their vehicles, then walk along the lane. There are security lights in the trees, installed since the accident.

'You do know I can never return to my seat,'

Dad says. 'There can be no forgiveness for what I've done.'

'I didn't say there was,' I tell him. 'That's not what I meant. What's important to you, Dad?'

We wander along the lane, hands in pockets. Above us, the sun is breaking through the clouds.

'Mum, Saffi . . . you.'

'What else?'

He pauses. 'I don't quite . . .'

I try to explain myself. 'We've heard you make lots of speeches, Dad. You were always slick.'

'That doesn't sound like a compliment.'

I shrug. 'It did the job, I suppose. It's what people expected. You always carried the crowd with you.'

He laughs. 'Do I sense a but coming?'

'Do you know when I heard you speak from the heart, I mean really speak from the heart? It was when you made that acceptance speech.'

'Where are you going with this, Nicky?'

Where am I going with it?

'Did you mean it? I have to know.'

He looks surprised, shocked even.

'Yes,' he answers, 'of course I meant it. Do you know it's about the only time I departed from the script? My minders didn't like that.' He glances at me. 'You wish I'd done it more often, don't you?'

I nod. 'Why couldn't you always do it? Do you remember when we visited the injured soldiers?'

'Yes, of course I do.'

'The stuff you said to them, it wasn't scripted, was it? That wasn't . . . politics?'

'No, Nick, I was talking as a soldier and as a man. Those guys, they were my brothers. Christ, how did I ever let them down?'

'Why did you?'

'Do you know what happens?' he says. 'You end up in a club, a tribe. If you want to do well, you accept its rules. What matters is not letting the other side win. It doesn't take long before you stop speaking for yourself and start singing from the party hymn sheet. That's politics, the art of the possible.' He shakes his head. 'Or maybe it's the art of the impossible. You lose yourself. You become another person.'

We've reached the oak tree. I run my fingers over the scarring on the bark.

'I nearly died here. There were times in that hospital bed when I *was* dead. I was breathing, but it felt as if life was over.'

'You didn't want to come back, did you?'

'No.'

'But you did come back, Nicky. Life found a way.' He gazes up at the dappled light playing in the treetops. 'So what's my way back?'

When I don't answer, he fixes me with a stare.

'OK, I have a question for you,' he says. 'I almost ripped this family apart with my lies. Do you think you can ever forgive me? I'm still the same person, you know.'

There was a time in that hospital room when I didn't believe that. But what happens to all the other stuff when you do something wrong? Does that die? Does that become nothing? The man who taught me to swim, ride a bike, march in his footsteps, the man who carried a comrade to safety under fire, the man who was a hero, was his past scrubbed away and made nothing by that one mistake?

'I can never forget,' I say.

'I see.'

'But I can forgive.'

He reaches in his pocket and feels the notes he made for his statement to the press.

'This part of my life is over,' he says. 'It's done.'

He tears the pieces of paper and lets them fly like confetti. I meet his gaze and tilt my head.

He nods and leads the way back to the house.

∎

I take out my phone to call Maria. Tonight, I will sleep deeply for the first time in many weeks.

There will be no pain.

The man with the dead eyes will stay away.

Read on for a preview of Alan's next book,

THE ISIS TRAP

THE PAST

SUMMER, 2014

There were three of them, squatting uneasily on the stone-littered, reddish-brown soil while the sun blazed down. There was no mercy in the heat of the Syrian afternoon. Sweat beaded the faces of the prisoners, who had their heads bowed, hands bound behind their backs. Dark emerald cypress trees stood to attention like servile guards flanking the figure of a young gunman. He was tall and lean, his oversized combat jacket hanging loosely on his slight frame.

'Well, Majid,' his commander chuckled, 'what do we do with these three? Any thoughts?'

Majid stared blankly at the man everybody knew as Omar. He was short and wiry with shaggy, black hair and a thick, untrimmed beard. There was a hidden meaning prowling behind his words.

'You look confused, Majid. Have you forgotten what they are doing here? Look at them. They bore arms against us.'

Omar kicked at their abandoned weapons and Majid instinctively raised his XM15 semi-automatic rifle to his chest, as if presenting it for inspection. What was he meant to do? Omar was still trying to prise the correct response out of his young comrade.

'In taking sides against the mujahideen of the Islamic State, they have declared themselves apostates. They are false Muslims. Don't you agree, Majid?'

For just a moment, Majid's gaze strayed to his left as he examined the faces of his fellow fighters. They were outwardly impassive, but he could read the raw fright in their eyes. He had fought alongside the captured men. He saw them as comrades in a common struggle.

'Did they not turn their weapons on us, Majid?'

Majid remembered the sudden firefight as a messy dispute about territory, an outbreak of hostilities with no clear cause, no obvious right or wrong. He had been hoping it would be easily resolved. What was the point of brothers' blood being shed in anger? One of Omar's most trusted fighters was leaning against a lone chinaberry tree, recording the scene with a hand-held camcorder. Now Majid got it. This was a test. He nodded briefly.

'Did they not kill two of your comrades?'

The answer was yes. Their bodies lay barely twenty metres away, crumpled on the parched earth, eyes staring up at the sky.

'Then you know what to do.'

Majid mustered a protest. 'I came here to heal, not to kill my brothers.'

'Only God can truly heal, Majid. If you want to save lives, you must do what is necessary.'

A man at the back of the group murmured something inaudible. Omar turned. His finger stroked the trigger of his automatic weapon.

'Something to say?'

There was no reply. Only a fool would argue with Omar. He stared at the watching fighters, eyes alive with pent-up rage. Everybody knew Omar was pressing Majid's buttons, trying to get a reaction, but they didn't know why. The scene was still being recorded. Omar turned his attention back to Majid.

'Is there a problem?'

By way of reply, Majid pressed the muzzle of his rifle against the back of the first captive's head.

'No problem.'

He knew that to refuse Omar was to die. Majid struggled to keep his grip firm. His hand was shaking. His mind screamed, but he dared not put his thoughts into words. Majid's finger was still lingering over the trigger when something attracted his attention, a silvery grey dart in the flawless, azure sky. The roar of an engine alerted the men to one of the regime's MiG-29 jet fighters.

The first of the aircraft's rockets was on its way before anyone could move. Flame flickered in the trail of dark smoke. There was the chatter of small arms fire and cries of 'Allahu Akbar' then the world exploded in smoke and fire. Like a tidal wave, a blast of raw energy swept over the landscape. An ear-splitting thunderclap announced a direct hit on the fighters' exposed position. The camera recording the scene continued to run.

When the smoke cleared not one man was left standing.

THE PRESENT

1

WEDNESDAY, 29TH JUNE

Amir is alone. He has got used to his own company. After all, what is the alternative? This is what his dad means by a new start, life without his friends. He has lived in a bubble of resentment for over a year now, as the family moved from flat to dingy flat. A crow distracts him, flapping clumsily over the yard then vanishing over the rooftops. He notices the boy in the black hoodie, sagging against the chain-link fencing. They are in the same set for English and Maths.

What are you looking at? Amir wonders. *Do you know something?*

Nikel has been watching Amir for some time. He wants to come over, but he is shy. His school uniform is dry-cleaned, his tie neatly knotted. Most of the kids have theirs pulled loose in protest at the school's latest attempt to impose a dress code. Yes, Nikel's a good boy, follows the rules, obeys his parents. Amir's dad would approve.

'Do you want something?'

Nikel looks startled.

'Well, do you?'

Nikel shrugs and comes over, takes a seat on the bench next to Amir and turns to look at him.

'You've been here a couple of months.'

Amir pulls a face. 'Observant, aren't you?' 'But you don't join in. You keep yourself to yourself.'

It's Amir's turn to stare.

'Right. I like my own company.'

'No, I don't think that's it.'

Amir's brow crumples. 'What's with you? Since when do you decide what I do or don't think?'

Nikel stands with his hands in his pockets. 'I've been watching you.'

Nikel's calm response wrong-foots Amir.

'Are you some kind of amateur detective? I told you, I keep myself to myself.'

By now, there's the hint of a smile playing around Nikel's mouth, as if he can read minds.

'I've seen you watching the other kids. You're the sociable type, but all this time you've been on the edge of things. Your sister's making friends. No, something is holding you back. Am I warm?'

The crow is back. Amir avoids Nikel's gaze.

'You don't know a thing about me.'

'Right,' Nikel answers. 'I don't, but you're not used to being a loner, I can tell that much.'

'How do you come to that conclusion, Sherlock?'

'Because I *am* a loner. I recognise the type, and you're not it.'

Amir leans back and considers Nikel.

'You're weird, you know that?'

Nikel chuckles. 'So people say.' He flicks a glance across the yard to a group of girls. Two of them are wearing hijab. A third is white, with strawberry blonde hair whipping in the wind.

'So you're twins, right, you and Nasima?'

He is nodding in the direction of the tallest girl.

'That's right, Nas is fifteen minutes older than me. She thinks she is ten years wiser.' Amir folds his arms in a show of mock suspicion. 'Fancy her, do you?'

'What if I did?'

'Oh, I'd have to kick the crap out of you. You're not Muslim.'

'How do you know that?'

'Just do.' He makes a series of passes with his hands. 'We have a secret sign, like the Freemasons.'

Nikel watches Amir's expression then laughs and punches his arm.

'That's a wind-up. You invented it.'

Amir grins.

'Had you going for a minute though, didn't I? I'd still kick your head in if you made a move on my sister.'

'Because I'm not Muslim?'

'Nah, because you're a freak of nature, geek boy.'

Amir considers Nikel. 'So what's your background? Indian?'

'British.'

'Yeah, yeah, we're all British. You know what I'm asking. What about your parents?'

'British.'

'Oh, come on, give me a break. What's your . . .' Inverted-comma fingers. '. . . heritage.'

Nikel gives in.

'My grandparents came from India. Goa.'

'So you're Hindu – elephant-headed gods and all that?'

'Catholic.'

'No way! In India?'

There's a gust of wind and Nikel zips up his jacket.

'Yes, it's a Portuguese thing. They settled, generations back, and brought their religion with them.'

'I thought Goa was hippies and beach barbecues. People with bells round their necks, dancing barefoot on the sand.'

'It's got that reputation.'

Amir can see that Nikel is plucking up the courage to ask another question.

'Go on, spit it out. What's on your mind?'

'How come you moved at this time of year? I mean, it's a bit close to exams to start a new school.'

Amir has told the truth once before. It meant the

family had to move on, in search of anonymity.

'Were you born nosy?' Amir asks, surprised that he doesn't feel angrier about the way Nikel is interrogating him.

'Probably. So what's the answer?'

Amir laughs.

'You're not getting one.'

Because answers mean danger.

Nikel considers his refusal.

'Fair enough.' Then, without so much as a pause, he moves on. 'Heard about what happened to that newsagent round the corner?'

Amir doesn't respond. Nikel ploughs on regardless.

'England Awakes kicked his head in the other night.'

'How do you know it was them?'

'They were shouting while they were beating him.' Nikel is watching Amir's expression. 'So, England Awakes: you've heard of it?'

Amir sees angry men, Union flags, the cross of St George. 'I don't live on Mars. Too right wing for the EDL. Too ugly for TV. This newsagent: how badly was he hurt?' 'Broken ribs. Fractured wrist. I smell trouble. There's a march at the weekend. Saturday. They've been spraying slogans on walls. *Torch the mosque*, that sort of thing.' He expects an answer. There isn't one. 'Anyway, the streets are going to be in lock-down. The council says the mosque can expand. England Awakes has got a campaign against it: Dump the Dome.'

Amir refuses to be drawn.

'Catchy.'

'Don't you care? They put the guy in hospital.'

'Seriously, what's it got to do with me?'

'You're Muslim. They're targeting your mosque. I thought you'd be raging.'

The bell rings to announce the end of lunchtime. Amir gets to his feet. 'Who cares, so long as they leave me alone?'

At that moment three boys jostle their way through the crush. Nikel watches them then drops his eyes when they turn his way. Amir registers the group.

'I'm guessing they're not fans of multiculturalism.'

Nikel rolls his eyes, lets the group pass and sets off towards the main building.

'Got it in one. A piece of advice: steer well clear.'